Who's Going to Love You But Me
Part II
- A Series Written by -
Melikia Gaino

Copyright © 2016 by True Glory Publications
Published by True Glory Publications LLC
Second Edition

This novel is a work of fiction. Any resemblances to actual events, real people, living or dead, organization, establishments, locales are products of the author's imagination. Other names, characters, places, and incidents are used fictitiously.

Cover design/Graphics:

Editor: Stormie Lynn

Because of the dynamic nature of the Internet, any Web addresses or links contained in this book may have changed since publication and may no longer be valid.

The views expressed in this work are solely those of the author and do not necessarily reflect the views of the publisher and the publisher hereby disclaims any responsibility for them.

Table of Contents

Chapter 1

Destiny...

As soon as Destiny saw Mya on the ground, she ran to her and held her. "Wake up Mya." Destiny cried while checking her pulse. "You still have a pulse, so you alive. Now open your eyes for me please Mya." Destiny said rocking her softly.

Mya could hear her but couldn't open her eyes. She reached for her hand and gave it a squeeze, letting her know she could hear her.

"She's going to be fine, but we have to get her to the doctors. She's pregnant." Destiny told Scott and Shad who both looked shocked.

"Pregnant?" Shad said, almost whispering it.

"Yes, now please help me carry her so we can get her to the hospital." Destiny said making a move to get up with Mya.

Shad wasted no time picking Mya's limp body up off the floor, ignoring the blood leaking everywhere. All he cared about was her safety. Carefully placing her in the car, they all piled in and headed to the hospital. Shad kept Mya's head on his lap while they drove, hoping that she would be ok. As soon as they got to the hospital, Mya was rushed in the back. Destiny told the nurses she was her sister and filled out the paper work.

"Where is your brother Scott?" Destiny asked pissed off. She knew that when she saw Kyle, she was going to split his shit for not being there.

"I don't know baby. Do you think we should call her mother or somebody?" Scott asked sending a text to Kyle letting him know what happened and where they were at. They both moved to the waiting area and sat down.

"Her mother wouldn't care. I don't want to worry Laurel but I don't have Loyalty's number either." Destiny said resting her head on Scott's shoulder. Shad was pacing back and forth, nervous for Mya. He cared about her a lot and didn't want to see her hurt.

Waiting for 2 hours the doctor finally came out. "Adams family." Scott and Destiny stood up and walked to the doctor. He looked at the teens and wondered where the adult was.

"Um do you all have an adult or a parent present?" The doctor asked skeptically.

"We are 18 which makes us adults and that's her sister. So may you please Dr. Wells let us know how Mya is doing?" Scott said.

"Ok. Well Ms. Adams had several bruises over her body that has hemorrhaged; a swollen nose and she also suffered a miscarriage. She lost a lot of blood so we did a transfusion. She will have to stay her for at least a week to be monitored. She will be ok." Dr. Wells said, then looked back at the teens and asked "Do any of you have any idea how Ms. Adams got the bruises on her body?"

They all had assumptions but didn't say anything so they all said no.

"Can I see her?" Destiny asked.

"Sure. We moved her to the 4th floor in room 420." Dr. Wells said pointing to the elevators.

They all rode the elevator up in silence, each lost in their own thoughts. When they made it to Mya's room, Destiny could barely recognize her with all the tubes coming out of her. She turned to Scott and said "I know your brother beat her."

"Baby you don't know that." Scott said trying to defend his brother.

"I know and if I see him I'm going to beat his ass like he did my sister." Destiny said walking over to Mya and holding her hand.

The room was quiet until Destiny's phone rang. It was Tamera calling.

"Hello." Destiny answered.

"Where you at? We have been waiting for you and Scott."

"We at the hospital. Mya's been admitted." Destiny said sadly.

"WHAT! We on our way." Tamera said hanging up.

After 20 minutes of being in the room and everyone in their own thoughts, Mya moved and opened her eyes.

"Hey." She said weakly.

"Mya you scared the shit out of me." Destiny said hugging her immediately. Mya groaned in pain causing Destiny to jump back away from her. "I'm so sorry. Did Kyle do this to you?"

Mya looked at Destiny and wanted to tell her the truth. She knew that she should have, but she didn't want her judging her relationship.

"No, I actually got in a fight with some girl that said she was sleeping with him three days ago."

Destiny didn't believe her but she didn't want to press the issue at the moment.

"Why would you fight her if you knew you were pregnant?" Shad quizzed. He knew her story wasn't adding up.

Mya looked at Shad and saw the love in his eyes for her but she was still stuck on protecting Kyle.

"I wasn't thinking at that moment." Mya said looking down at her hands.

Shad walked over to the bed grabbed her hand and kissed it. He looked her straight in the eyes and said "Don't do anything like that again that will threaten your life."

Mya looked deep in his light brown eyes and said "I won't." Just when she looked away from him, her room door opened to more people coming in, including Lord.

He walked over to the bed like a big brother and asked her "What the fuck happened?"

Mya explained about her "fight" with the other girl and told them she was pregnant and lost the baby.

"Why the fuck were you fighting over that nigga anyway Mya? Especially pregnant." Lord said shaking his head at her.

"Lord I didn't think about it." Mya said.

"Yea, where is that bitch ass nigga at anyway?" Lord asked getting mad.

Before anyone could reply, Kyle came in the room and looked around. He saw Lord standing on one side of Mya's bed and Shad on the other. He screwed up his face at the sight. He looked them both up and down and then looked at Mya.

"Baby I'm sorry I took so long. Are you ok?" Kyle said walking up to her pushing Shad out the way.

Mya looked at him with a little fear in her eyes and answered him in a weak voice, "I'm ok."

"Where the fuck was you at when she was at home almost bleeding to death?" Destiny asked ready to attack him but Scott grabbed her up before she could reach him.

Kyle looked at her with a death glare and said "If you must know Ms. Destiny, I was making money. I didn't have my phone on so I wasn't able to know she called but I got Scott text message once I turned my phone on."

"Don't you think if you gonna fuck around on Mya, you need to keep your chicks in order?" Lord said, eyeing him angrily.

"What the fuck are you talking about nigga?" Kyle asked confused.

"The bitch that did this to my fucking best friend. The chick said she was fucking you and they fought." Lord said heated now.

Kyle looked over to Mya. He was happy inside that she covered for him, but was pissed that her friends were in their business. Turning his attention back to Lord, he looked him up and down. "Nigga don't worry about our relationship. Bitches be out here lying. I told Mya don't be feeding into that bullshit."

"Yo I should just fuck you up right now." Lord said making a step in Kyle's direction.

"Mya check your boy. I already told you I don't like you around this nigga any way." Kyle said ready to meet him.

"Calm down Lord please." Mya said weakly while pushing him back.

"Calm down Mya? You scared of this nigga or something. Fuck that bitch ass nigga. You know what, I love you. You always gonna be my best friend and sister, but since you listening to this nigga about not being around me and shit I'll leave. Holla at me when you realize this nigga ain't shit but bad news. Get better baby girl." Lord said kissing her forehead and walking out.

Shad looked over at Kyle trying to portray the supporting boyfriend and got pissed. "I'm out. Feel better Mya." Shad said looking at her then turned to Destiny and Scott "I'll wait for y'all outside."

Everyone started to walk out the room leaving Scott, Destiny, Mya and Kyle.

"You need me to stay with you Mya?" Destiny asked.

"I'm fine Destiny. I know ma is gonna be worried about you." Mya said looking down at her hands. Times like this, she wish she could depend on her own mother.

"I texted her and told her where I was. I'll be back tomorrow then." Destiny said leaning in to hug Mya's shoulder.

"Ok. Love you." She said, embracing her back.

"Love you too." Destiny said

Scott told her to feel better and gave his brother a look of disgust as he followed Destiny out the room. Walking down the hall, Destiny looked at Scott and said "I hope you never put your hands on me."

"I would never do that." Scott said pulling her into a hug as they got on the elevator.

"Good, because I have uncle who will kill you after I beat your ass." Destiny said with a straight face.

Scott leaned down and kissed her on the lips while laughing, causing Destiny to smile in return.

Chapter 2

Laurel...

After Laurel's talk with Loyalty about being home sick, she decided to finish all her assignments and finals early so she could go home for summer break. Before she left, she put all her stuff in storage and hit the road. No one knew she was coming home, not even Loyalty. She wanted to surprise him and her friends. The drive from Massachusetts wasn't bad. She planned on seeing Loyalty, then going to see her girls and track her damn sister down. Pulling up to her and Loyalty's condo, she parked in her space, grabbed her suitcase and headed to the door. When she walked in, he was on the couch sleep with only basketball shorts on. She stood and admired him, loving the view in front of her. Pulling out her phone from her purse, she snapped a picture of him. Walking up on him, she leaned down and kissed his lips softly.

"I better be dreaming, because if I open my eyes and it's my homesick girlfriend, I'm going to teach her a lesson for dipping out on school." Loyalty said with his eyes still closed.

Laurel held in her laughter and hid behind the couch when Loyalty finally opened his eyes.

"You might as well come out from behind the couch because I have a six sense when it comes to you." Loyalty said, stretching his arms.

Laurel stood up and leaned over the couch into him. Wrapping her arms around his neck, she started to kiss on his cheek and neck.

"Don't try and butter a nigga up with those soft lips of yours." Loyalty said pulling her over the couch and putting her on his lap.

"I'm not buttering you up. I've just missed you a lot."

"I thought we talked about you coming home next week for summer break. You better not be dipping on any classes." Loyalty said while playing with her clit through her sweat pants.

"I know, but the professors let me do all my finals and assignments early so I could leave." Laurel moaned out, loving the feeling of his hand between her legs.

"What your grades looking like?" Loyalty asked sucking on her neck.

"They will post tomorr… mmmmm." Laurel moaned when he moved his hand inside her pants. Loyalty massaged her clit with one hand, while pulling her pants down with the other.

"Good. Let's make these babies." Loyalty said stripping Laurel of all her clothes.

Laurel was in heaven as her and Loyalty made love on the couch. After having multiple orgasms they both showered and got dressed.

"So what you have planned today?" Loyalty asked as he tied his shoe laces.

"I'm going around the way to see the girls and then go find my sister. What about you?" Laurel said pulling her boyshorts on.

"I have a couple of pickups to do and then I'm going to find my wife so we can find our little sister.

I'm going to take my ladies out to dinner and then you and I are going to continue making babies." Loyalty said walking over to her and kissing her on the lips.

"I like that plan." Laurel said biting her lip when he pulled away.

"Well let's be out."

They both got in their separate cars and headed to their destinations. Laurel pulled up around her way a short time later. Since everyone was out of school already, it was packed outside. She spotted Tiara and Melanie talking on the stoop and walked up to them.

"So this is what y'all do when school is over." Laurel said. They both looked at her and screamed.

"Oh my gooodnessssss! We missssed your ass so much!" Tiara yelled as she stood to hug Laurel.

"I missed y'all too. So what's been up?" Laurel asked sitting on the stoop with them.

"Girl, since your brother got locked that nigga Cash been running round here like he the Godfather or some shit. Like he really gangsta now. Other than that, shit been mellow." Melanie said.

"So, have y'all seen my mom?" Laurel asked looking up at the window of her old apartment.

"Yea. We saw Ms. Liz. She looks the same and shit." Tiara said shrugging.

"What about Mya?" Laurel asked anxiously.

Melanie and Tiara looked at each other but didn't want to be the one to tell Laurel about her sister.

"Can one of you tell me what's up with my sister?" Laurel said impatiently. She could see it on their faces that something was up.

"Ok. Tamara came home a couple of days ago and told me that Mya was in the hospital. She said she got in a fight with one of Kyle chicks. She was pregnant and lost it..." Before Tiara could continue Laurel cut her off.

"Hold the fuck up. You telling me that my sister is in the hospital and neither one of you ain't call and tell me." Laurel said pissed off.

"I called you when I found out, but you seemed like you was on the verge of a breakdown your damn self. I couldn't put that stress on you." Tiara said trying to make Laurel see reason.

Laurel knew Tiara didn't tell her to look out for her health, but she still was pissed.

"What hospital?" Laurel asked.

"Greater Southeast."

Laurel got up and walked to the car without saying anything. When she got in, she called Loyalty.

"Dang babe you just left a nigga. You miss me already?" Loyalty joked once he answered the phone.

"Baby, Mya is in the hospital." Laurel said trying not to cry.

"What? Which one?" Loyalty asked while turning his car in the opposite direction of where he was going.

"Greater Southeast." Laurel said, holding the phone and speeding to the hospital.

"I'm on my way." Loyalty said hanging up.

Laurel pulled up at the hospital parking lot and got out. She ran to the front desk and got the nurses attention. "I'm looking for my sister Mya Adams." Laurel said trying to catch her breath.

"She's in room 402."

"Thank you." Laurel said running for the elevators and getting on. She walked to Mya's room when she reached the 4th floor and slowly pushed the door open. Her eyes zoning in on the bed, she saw that Mya was sleeping peacefully. She walked over to her bed and took a seat in the chair next to it. She grabbed Mya's hand, causing her to open her eyes.

"Laurel?" Mya asked in a low voice.

"It's me Mya." Laurel said smiling at her.

"Oh my God. I miss you so much." Mya said smiling and then starting to cry.

"I miss you too." Laurel said crying as well, pulling her into a hug.

They both were hugging each other and crying. Destiny had just walked in the room when she saw them. Not wanting to interrupt their moment, she stood at the door. They finally broke their hug when they heard "I don't need no fucking pass. My sister is in that fucking room."

Mya and Laurel looked at each other and said "Loyalty."

"Hey y'all. Didn't want to interrupt the moment." Destiny said once they looked at her standing by the door.

"Looking good little sis." Laurel said to Destiny as she walked over to them.

"Looking good yourself big sis." Destiny said giving Laurel a hug then passing Mya the food she went and got her.

Loyalty finally came in the room with Moss and Kelly behind him.

"Yo, fucking rent-a-cops blow the shit out of me." Loyalty said

Mya smiled when she saw all of the people she considered family in the room.

"Damn sis. You needed a break from that nigga that bad that you had to come to the hospital?" Moss said causing everyone to laugh.

"Shut up Moss." Mya said laughing.

"On the real. What happened to you?" Loyalty asked when the laughter died down.

"Um." Mya began. She always felt like she couldn't lie to Laurel and Loyalty. They always knew if she was being truthful.

"Ummm what? We waiting." Loyalty said.

"Some girl came to me and said she was sleeping with Kyle. We got into a fight and I was pregnant. She kicked me in my stomach and made me have a miscarriage." Mya said not making eye contact with them.

"Again Mya. Stop fighting over that piece of shit nigga. What he had to say about it? Matter of fact, where he is?" Laurel asked, waving her arm around the room.

"He had some business to handle. He told me to stop believing these girls out here." Mya said still not making eye contact.

Loyalty didn't say anything. He just looked at Mya knew she was lying. Before anyone else could say anything the doctor walked in.

"Hello Ms. Adams. I see you have a full house today." Dr. King said, taking in the new faces in the room.

"Yea Dr. King. That's my older sister Laurel and my brother in law." Mya said pointing to Laurel and Loyalty.

Dr. King shook Loyalty and Laurel hands and then moved to check Mya's vitals.

"Everything is looking good Ms. Adams."

"Thank you." Mya said.

Loyalty and Laurel followed Dr. King out of the room.

"Hey doc can we talk to you for a second." Loyalty said walking up to the doctor as he turned around.

"Sure, what can I do for you all?"

"What really happened to my little sister?" Loyalty asked. He was going to find out the truth, one way or another.

"Well when she came in through the emergency room, she had several bruises over her body and she lost a lot of blood due to the miscarriage. She had to have a transfusion. Upon her coming to, we asked where the bruising came from and she said she was in a fight." The doctor explained.

"So how long will she be in here?" Laurel asked.

"Well when your other sister filled the paperwork out, she didn't put any insurance. She is actually doing better, so we might have to discharge her in the next two days.

We really need her to stay longer to monitor her blood pressure though. She also had swelling around her brain which was another concern for us."

"Don't worry about the cost. I will pay the bill. Just make sure my sister is perfect before she leaves." Loyalty said.

"Well do sir." The doctor said shaking Loyalty's hand.

Laurel and Loyalty spent the whole day with Mya after their talk with her doctor. In the back of their minds, they knew Kyle was responsible for Mya being in the hospital. It was only a matter of time before they got their hands on him.

__*__*__

Mya...

Mya woke up and looked around at her empty room. Laurel and Loyalty spent the whole day with her and she could honestly say she missed them so much. She looked to the night stand and saw a note in her sister's hand writing.

Mya,

You fell asleep on us so we went home to get some rest. I will be back in the morning to see you with your favorite breakfast: French toast and bacon. Oh and when you get discharged, you coming and living with us. No, if, ands or buts.

Love you sis

Laurel

Mya just laughed at the note. She knew her sister was serious about her living with them.

"What got you smiling so hard?" Kyle said walking in the room.

"Oh, just a note my sister wrote me. She is home for summer break and came to see me." Mya said.

"Oh." Kyle said not liking the idea of her and her sister back in contact. He knew if Laurel was around again, she would stop Mya from seeing him.

"So, how everything been?" Mya asked changing the subject.

"Busy, but my money not coming up right like when I got you on my side." Kyle said kissing her cheek.

Mya smiled and said "I will be back on your arm in no time."

"That's what I need to hear." Kyle said smirking. He knew he had Mya where he wanted her.

"My sister wants me to move with her when I get out the hospital." Mya told him, looking down at her hands.

Kyle screwed his face up and looked at her. "Is this your way to tell me you leaving me or something?"

"No, I was just letting you know." Mya said starting to get nervous.

"Are you going with her?" Kyle asked, moving closer to her bed.

Mya looked at him and saw the fear of losing her in his eyes.

"No, I'm staying with you." Mya said, trying to please him.

Kyle smiled down at her. He leaned over and kissed her passionately on the lips.

"I love you Mya." Kyle said looking in her eyes.

"I love you too Kyle."

"Let's leave here now. I hate hospitals." Kyle said pulling her sheets back.

"I'm not sure if I can leave now." Mya said looking up at him.

"I'm going to go get the doctor and if they say you good to go, are we leaving?" Kyle asked already knowing the answer.

"Yes." Mya said reluctantly.

Kyle went and got the doctor. He came back shortly after and checked Mya out. Although he recommended bed rest and some prescriptions, he discharged her. The car ride home was quiet until Mya realized they were going in the wrong direction to their house.

"Kyle where are we going? We live the other way." Mya said looking at the scenery around her.

"It's a surprise baby." Kyle said holding her hand. They pulled up to a nice house and Kyle pulled in the drive way. They both got out and stood in front of the mini mansion. "Welcome home baby."

Mya smiled and remembered when she was younger and her family lived in a house like the one she was looking at before her father went to prison. "I love it." she said jumping in Kyle's arms and kissing him.

Laurel...

Laurel got off the elevator with food for Mya in her hand. When she pushed opened her door, she saw that the bed was empty as well as the room. Laurel went to the nurse's station to get information on her sister's whereabouts.

"Excuse me." Laurel said looking at the nurse on duty.

"Yes. How may I assist you?"

"Do you know if they moved Mya Adams to another room?"

The nurse looked her name up and said "Actually Ms. Adams was discharged this morning."

"What? Who signed? She is only 16." Laurel was on the verge of becoming hysterical.

"It says Kyle Johnson signed her out." The nurse said.

Laurel wanted to cry but she held it in and said "Thank you." When she left the hospital, got in her car and called Mya's phone.

"The number you are trying to reach has been disconnected."

Laurel hung up the phone and headed home. Loyalty was on the phone when Laurel walked in crying.

"My nig, I have to hit you back. Wifey is home." Loyalty said ending his call and walking Laurel. "What's wrong?" he asked while pulling her into his arms.

"She was gone. He discharged her and her phone is off." Laurel said crying harder. "I just want my family back, Loyalty. I miss them."

Loyalty held her while she cried. He was going to make it his goal to make Laurel's wish come true. All he wanted was for his future wife to be happy. Getting her family back was going to do it. He was willing to do what he had to do no matter how long it would take.

Chapter 3

2 years later

Two years had passed and so much had changed. After Laurel left the hospital and cried on Loyalty's shoulder, she woke up the next day and decided she wanted to finish college early. She wanted to marry Loyalty and move on with their lives. Deciding to go to summer school, she finished her undergraduate studies a year early and was now in her first year of law school at Harvard. Loyalty would visit her all the time when she didn't fly home. He was still in the process of getting her family back together again. He hired the top lawyers to work on her father's and brother's case. He was even paying Liz visits to get to know her better. The only hard thing was finding Mya. Kyle really had a hold on her. He had been trying to find out where she lived now, with no such luck.

Destiny and the girls had graduated from high school without Mya, even though it was weird to not have all four of them together to walk across the stage, they managed. Destiny was determined to leave DC and no one was stopping her. She was accepted and going to Spelman in Atlanta while Scott was going to attend Le Cordon Bleu College of Culinary Arts Atlanta. Even with the distance and strain on Mya's and Destiny's friendship, she was always thinking about Mya. Destiny would get a call out of the blue from Mya from time to time to let them know she was doing ok, since she didn't have a way to get in contact with her unless she called. She would always tell her to come stay with her, but she would always decline the offer. Shad still thought about Mya all the time but was now a sophomore at Johnson C. Smith University studying business. He didn't take a year off like his boys since he didn't have a girl to wait for. He just wanted to leave DC and start fresh.

He was no longer Lil Shad, now he was a ladies man that every girl wanted, but the only girl he wanted to be his forever was in his past. Only thing he knew was that she still and forever have his heart.

Mya and Kyle's relationship was still the same. He stopped beating her for a little then it started back. Now Mya cope's with the pain by drinking.

Chapter 4

Mya...

Mya walked in the house from getting her hair done since Kyle told her they were going out that night.

"Where you been at?" Kyle asked.

"I went to go get my hair done. You said we going out tonight." Mya said alarmed.

"Didn't I tell you to call me when you leave this fucking house?" Kyle said coming towards her. Mya's back was up against the door as Kyle stood over her.

"I did call you but you didn't answer."

"Don't that mean stay your dumb ass in the house Mya?" Kyle questioned.

Mya didn't say anything.

"Bitch I know you hear me talking to you." He said, pushing her shoulder.

Keeping her head lowered, she replied, "Yes."

Next thing Mya knew, she tasted copper. Kyle had smacked her so hard across the face, blood insistently came from her mouth. He didn't stop with smacking her. He punched and kicked her over and over. All Mya could do was take the beating she was receiving. Once Kyle got tired he looked down at her. "You make me do this shit to you. Now your ass has to stay in the house." Kyle said walking out the door, leaving her on the floor beaten and bloody.

Mya pulled herself off the floor and slowly walked to bathroom. She looked in the mirror and was disappointed by what she saw. The person looking back at her was no longer the feisty, beautiful, confident Mya Adams. This girl looking at her was a battered, scared, unloved woman. Mya used to have curves, skin that glows and sparkling eyes that were full of life. Now she was thin, with dark dull eyes, and paleness to her skin.

"Who are you?" Mya asked herself while staring in the mirror. Cleaning herself up, she went to her room and looked at the pictures she hid from Kyle. It was a picture of her and her family, and another one of her and her friends that she missed so much. She picked up her phone and dialed Destiny's number.

"Hello." Destiny answered on the 3rd ring.

"Hey Destiny." Mya said hearing a lot of noise in her background.

"Is this my sister from another mister?" Destiny asked causing Mya to laugh.

"Of course it is. Is this a bad time?"

"It's my going away party. I'm still lost as to why you not here."

"I totally forgot Des, I'm so sorry. I wanted to call and tell you I love you and live it up in ATL." Mya said sadly.

Mya didn't forget about the party. She wanted to be there but Kyle told her if she stepped foot back in her old neighborhood, he would kill her.

"It's ok. I love you too and I will. Maybe you will come and visit me." Destiny said hopefully.

"I plan on it. Have fun. I will call you when I can."

"Ok." Destiny said even though she didn't want to hang up. She knew Mya was in danger and every time she tried to help her she don't want the help. She kept saying everything was ok.

Mya hung up with Destiny. Looking at the photo of her and her family, she stared at them smiling. Phone in hand, she dialed Laurel's number but blocked her number from being seen. While the phone was ringing, she was having second thoughts. She started to hang up when the other line picked up.

"Hello." Laurel said skeptically.

Mya didn't know what to say, so she kept quiet on her end. It's been two years since she talked to her sister and she was scared that she would be mad at her.

"Hello." Laurel said again impatiently.

"I'm sorry Laurel." Mya cried into the phone. "I love you."

"Mya?" Laurel said on the verge of tears.

"It's me."

"I've been worried about you. Are you ok?" Laurel asked. She desperately wanted to see her.

"I'm sorry for making you worry. I'm ok." Mya said. She knew Kyle was home when she heard a car pull into the drive-way. "Laurel I love you. I will call you another time. I have to go." Mya said hanging up.

Kyle walked in the house and went to their room. When he walked in, he saw Mya on the bed with an ice pack on her cheek.

"Look, I'm sorry for doing that to you. Do you still love me?" Kyle asked handing her a small opened box. In it was a shining gold diamond necklace.

"Yes I still love you." Mya said carefully taking the box from his hands.

Mya was so used to this routine. He beat her, make her clean herself up, come home with a gift, ask do she still love him, she say yes, they have make up sex. When she started to heal some, he would end up doing the shit all over again.

"That's my girl." Kyle said kissing her while pushing her back on the bed. Mya was so tired of this relationship but didn't know how to get out. The sex was the same every time too. He would be rough with her, cum and then make her shower. As expected, after the 15 minutes of Kyle pounding her, he came in her and then told her to get in the shower.

Mya walked out the shower in a towel and saw Kyle fully dressed to head to the club. She already knew she wasn't going out the house with her face looking the way it did.

"Look Mya I'm going to the club. I'll see you later." Kyle said kissing her forehead and leaving out.

"Ok, be safe." Mya said, happy to be rid of him for the time being. As soon as the door closed and Mya was alone, she went to her best friend: the vodka bottle. As she drunk the vodka, she became numb and dreamed she was in a better, happier place.

Chapter 5

Kyle...

Kyle had the music up loud as he drove to Zanzibar Nightclub. He was meeting up with his boys, knowing that the night would be epic. It was only right to pop bottles in VIP and have bad bitches surrounding him. Kyle parked his car in the front of the club and walked right in towards VIP. When he got in, he saw his boys Taye, Slim and Pete with bottles in front of them.

"Nigga took your ass long enough." Slim said facing a bottle of Ace of Spades.

"Fuck you nigga." Kyle said grabbing a bottle of Ace from the ice.

"Where is sis? I thought she was coming out with you?" Taye asked not seeing Mya with him.

"Fuck you asking about my woman fo' nigga?" Kyle asked looking at Taye like he was crazy.

"Nigga chill the fuck out. I was just seeing where she at. Don't nobody want Mya ass."

"Whatever. I left her ass at home. She was doing too much." Kyle said taking a sip from the bottle.

"In other words you beat her ass and she had to stay home." Pete said laughing while holding his bottle.

Kyle just smirked not saying anything. Taye shook his head at the situation. He hated that Kyle beat on Mya so much.

He felt that no man should put his hands on a woman he claimed to "love".

His thoughts cleared when a few girls came over to their section and started dancing on them. Grabbing his bottle, he drank some while a girl gave him a lap dance.

__*__*__

Loyalty…

"Nigga why you got me in this club?" Loyalty asked Kelly as he looked around Zanzibar. He didn't feel like being out on the scene tonight. He actually wanted to be home in bed getting rest so he could drive to Boston to see his woman.

"Lighten up. You gonna make it to see Laurel man. Plus this nigga Moss had to get out the house from crazy ass Tiara." Kelly said causing them to laugh.

"Fuck you nigga. My baby not crazy. She just… naw I'm lying like shit. She is crazy. Kirking off and everything. Nigga I had to change your name in my phone cause she see your fucking girly ass name and think you a female calling. I gotta tell her every time who it is." Moss said shaking his head.

"Damn, nigga. You sure her ass ain't pregnant again?" Loyalty asked. He knew when Tiara was pregnant before, she was doing some off the wall stuff.

"Shit I hope not. As much as I don't want to, I'm bout to start wrapping it up." Moss said shaking his head while downing some Henny.

"I'm glad my woman doesn't want any kids any time soon." Kelly said with relief.

Loyalty and Moss looked at each other and burst out laughing.

"What the fuck am I missing?" Kelly asked confused.

"Yo girl told Laurel that she is ready to have some babies." Loyalty said laughing hard. "She may have told you she didn't want any yet, but that was just to test you."

"Oh hell naw." Kelly said gulping his Henny down.

They stopped talking about their women and started to vibe to the music. Loyalty was looking around the club, when he spotted Kyle with some girl all up on him.

"Look who we have here." Loyalty said with a smirk. He took notice that the girl dancing on him wasn't Mya.

"Who?" Moss asked, looking around.

"That nigga Kyle." He replied with a smirk. "I'll be back." Loyalty got up and walked over to Kyle's VIP. He was so busy kissing on the girl's neck that he hadn't noticed him appear. Loyalty shook his head at how dumb he was. "Yo, let me talk to you fo' a second." Loyalty said to Kyle as he walked closer.

Kyle looked up from the girl's neck into Loyalty's face, "For what nigga? We ain't got shit to talk about."

Loyalty waved him off, "Look, all I wanna know is where my fucking sister is yo. Kill that fucking big boy act in front of your lil female."

"She is where she is. Don't be coming over here like you the king of this bitch." Kyle said stepping around the girl to get into Loyalty's face.

Loyalty looked him in the eye as he laughed him out, "You really have a lot of growing up to do lil nigga. Tell MY sister to fucking call me."

Smirking at him, he replied, "Not gonna happen. I'm the only family she need now."

"You really testing me. Let me go before I beat the shit out of you in this bitch." Loyalty said turning to walk away.

Kyle felt like he was being disrespected by his dismissal. He picked up a bottle and hit Loyalty across the back of the head with it. Loyalty saw red as he turned around and punched the shit out of Kyle, sending him flying back to the couches. What Kyle didn't know was that Loyalty had been boxing since he was 5 years old. Kyle didn't know what hit him as Loyalty jumped on him, raining punches left and right. Taye, Pete and Slim ran over but were met by Kelly and Moss who stopped them from coming closer.

"I don't think that's a good idea to jump in that." Moss said with his hand up.

Taye knew how Moss, Loyalty and Kelly got down. He kept telling Kyle to stop playing with them.

"Back down y'all." Taye said knowing this was something they couldn't interfere with.

Moss saw the bouncers coming and went to Loyalty.

"Let's go bruh. You about to kill that nigga." Moss said trying to pull him up off Kyle.

"Fuck that bitch. Imma kill him." Loyalty said pulling his gun out. He cocked it and aimed it straight for Kyle's head.

Moss grabbed it fast and put the safety back on. "Not here. It's too many witnesses. Let's go."

Kelly settled the bill as they walked away from the scene. When they got outside, Loyalty reached back and touched the lump on the back of his head. Bringing his hand back, he saw blood coating his fingers.

"That bitch ass nigga hit me with a bottle. Fucked up my head." He said fuming.

"That was a bitch move for real." Moss said shaking his head. He should have known to not try and sneak attack.

Before Loyalty could respond, his phone rang. He looked at the time and knew it was Laurel calling. She usually left the library at that time and would call to talk.

"Hello." He answered trying to sound normal.

"What's wrong with you?" Laurel asked knowing him too well.

"Yo take me to the fucking hospital. This shit keeps bleeding." Loyalty said forgetting he was on the phone with Laurel for a second.

"Hospital! What the fuck is going on Loyalty?" Laurel yelled through the phone.

"Shit." Loyalty said realizing what he said on the phone then added "Baby chill out. Everything is alright."

"How is everything alright if you're heading to the hospital? Loyalty just tell me." Laurel said starting to cry.

Sighing, he passed the phone to Kelly who was in the back of the car. He couldn't handle Laurel crying on the phone at that moment. They pulled up to the hospital and got out. Loyalty walked ahead of him to the emergency room.

"Hey Laurel stop crying ma. He just got into a fight but he straight. We at the hospital and he can't be on the phone. I'll keep you updated." Kelly said, trying to calm her down.

"Ok. Tell him I love him." Laurel said sniffling.

They were at the front desk and Loyalty was signing in.

"Yo, she said she love you." Kelly told Loyalty as he walked up to him with the phone in his hand.

Loyalty looked at him like he was stupid and snatched his phone.

"I love you too baby. I gotta go."

"Ok. Call me as soon as you leave."

"Ok." Loyalty said hanging up.

Mya...

Mya had just drunk herself to sleep when she heard the banging on her door.

"Hold on." Mya said getting out the bed in her night shorts and tank top and walking downstairs. "Who is it?" she asked, when she reached the front door.

"Taye." Mya opened the door and was shocked to see a badly beaten Kyle being held up.

"What happened to him Taye?" Mya asked following them to the living room.

"He got in a fight with your brother?" Taye said moving him to the couch.

"My brother? My brother is locked up." Mya said confused.

"Not Mike. Loyalty."

Mya was about to say something but Kyle interrupted her. "Bitch stop talking and get the shit to clean my fucking face up."

Mya jumped at the tone of his voice and ran from the room to get supplies.

"You didn't have to yell at her man." Taye said looking at his friend with disgust.

"Man, you getting soft out here. Fuck her feelings. I'm the one fucked up." Kyle said sitting up slowly.

"In case you haven't realized nigga, that's that karma that happened to you. You must didn't look at her face. You fucked her up and now her brother fucked you up. You need to check that shit." Taye said shaking his head at him.

Kyle was going to say something but Mya came back in with peroxide, water and a washcloth. Not wanting to anger him, she began to help clean his face up.

"I'm out. Take care sis. I'll see you later Kyle." Taye said walking out the front door.

Mya looked at Kyle and asked "Do you want to talk about it?"

"Just know your sister will be without a man soon." Kyle said getting up and leaving her downstairs.

Mya sat on the couch for a minute and was deep in thought when she heard the shower water running. Thinking quickly, she grabbed her phone, blocked her number, and dialed a number she knew by heart. The phone kept ringing, but Mya refused to hang up just yet. After the 5th ring, the person on the other line picked up.

"Who is this?"

"Loyalty, it's Mya."

"Sis, where the fuck are you?" Loyalty asked.

"Just know I'm safe. I was calling to let you know please watch your back and protect my sister." Mya said listening out for the shower water.

"What you talking about sis?"

"Kyle. He saying that he gonna kill you for beating him up." Mya said fast when she heard the shower cut off. "I have to go." Mya said hanging up and cutting her burner phone off and hiding it.

The bedroom door opened and Kyle yelled down, "Mya bring your ass up here."

Mya knew what her night was going to be like. She went into the kitchen and took a gulp of Vodka from her stash. Heading upstairs she knew her night had really just begun.

Chapter 6

Two months later…

Kyle's beatings were getting worse and worse to the point that Mya just was getting numb to it. She would no longer cry or pray to God and ask to get her away from Kyle. Now she felt like God abandoned her. She just took the beatings and would drink afterwards and go on about her day. Today wasn't any different. Only thing was that it was Kyle's birthday and he was having a dinner party.

Mya was getting ready when Kyle walked in, looking at her. She had covered up all the bruises and looked good, just thinner than she normally was.

"You look good." Kyle said kissing her cheek, causing Mya to flinch from the bruise she covered up with concealer.

"Thank you." Mya said giving him a weak smile.

They both walked to the limo outside that was taking them to the restaurant. In the car, Kyle kept rubbing on Mya's thigh and even though she was scared of him, it felt good for him to touch her in an intimate way.

"I love you Mya." Kyle said smiling over at her.

"I love you too Kyle." Mya said smiling at him.

Pulling up to the restaurant, all of Kyle's friends and their girls were there. Some of the girls from his neighborhood were there as well. Mya knew Kyle had slept with some of them if not all of them, but he would say they were just friends of his, making her feel uncomfortable.

"Happy birthday." Everyone yelled when he walked in.

"Thank you all." Kyle said dapping the dudes up and hugging the girls.

The girls that Mya liked she hugged. The ones she didn't like she didn't say anything to them as she passed by.

"Nigga your ass close to 25 now." Pete said as he dapped Kyle up.

"Yea man. A nigga getting old out here. Baby you don't mind your man getting old, do you?" Kyle asked, looking down into Mya's eyes.

She looked up at him and smiled. "No I don't mind."

"How you been Mya?" Taye asked keeping eye contact with her. He and Mya had grown to have a good bond over the years. Even though when they first met she didn't like him, he started to treat her like a little sister. Even his girlfriend Natalia understood their relationship. She got along great with Mya as well.

Mya smiled at Taye. "I've been good."

He knew she was lying but didn't say anything about it. "That's good."

Natalia noticed a bruise on Mya's wrist when she looked at her and tapped Taye.

"Why does he keep beating her?" Natalia whispered so that only Taye could hear her.

"I can't answer that baby. She is trapped and blinded by love ma."

"Mya girl, walk with me to the bathroom." Natalie said as she stood up from the table.

Mya looked at Kyle for permission and he gave her a nod on the low.

"Ok." Mya said grabbing her purse.

When they got inside the bathroom, Natalia wasted no time voicing her thoughts. "Mya, why do you keep letting him beat you?"

"What are you talking about?" Mya asked like she didn't know. She knew she covered all of the bruises up.

"Mya, you are like my sister. I see the mark on your arm." Natalia said pointing to a purple bruise near her wrist.

Mya looked down and sighed. She knew she was caught.

"It's not that easy to leave him. He controls everything I do." Mya said, starting to cry.

"Mya, get out of there before he ends up killing you." Natalia said hugging her.

"Where will I go? I haven't talked to my family in years. My best friend Destiny is in Atlanta. I don't have anyone but you and Taye. I can't come to y'all. He will find me and it will just be worse."

"Sis, I'm going to get you away from that nigga. Me and Taye will." Natalia said reassuring her.

"NO, I don't want y'all getting in the middle of this. I will be fine." Mya said pulling away from her. The less people involved the better.

Natalia knew she wouldn't leave until she was ready to leave. "Ok. Let's fix your make up."

After making sure her bruise was covered, they both headed back to the table.

"You good?" Kyle asked Mya when she sat down. He noticed her cheeks were a little pink.

"Yes I'm fine." Mya said smiling at him.

They ordered their food and drinks. Mya ordered a dirty martini since they didn't card her. She was on her third one by time the food came out.

"Slow the fuck down with the drinking." Kyle whispered in her ear, grabbing her thigh with force.

"Ok." Mya said wincing slightly from his grasp.

Kyle kissed her cheek. Throughout the rest of the dinner, Mya sipped her drink and didn't say anything. She tuned out the conversations around her. She thought of the times when she was happy, hanging with her girls, and Scott and his boys; Times when her, Laurel and Mike would hang out. Mya ignored the flirting Kyle was doing with the other girls in the restaurant since her mind was focused on other things.

"Yo, I know we clubbing it tonight." Slim said looking to Kyle for confirmation.

"Hell yea. Let's go." Kyle said paying for the bill when it arrived.

He and Mya got in the limo, while his friends got in their cars, heading to the club.

"Yo, when we get to this club, don't start all that fucking drinking. If your ass gets drunk, I'm fucking you up on site." Kyle said.

Mya looked over at him and just stared.

"You don't hear me talking to you?" Kyle asked after she didn't say anything.

"Ok, Kyle." Mya sighed out.

"Good." Kyle said grabbing her face and kissing her fully on the lips.

They pulled up to club Fix and went in, heading straight to VIP. Mya met up with Natalia and decided to get a drink and hit the dance floor. She knew that Kyle wasn't keeping an eye on her in the crowd, so she decided to enjoy herself and let loose. After dancing with Natalia for over an hour, she wants to go sit for a few.

"My feet are killing me. Let's go back upstairs." Mya suggested.

"Ok." Natalia said walking with her. Her feet were screaming for a little relief.

As they walked back up the stairs to VIP, Mya saw Kyle feeling up on a girl. It must have been the liquor in her system or the embarrassment that he was doing this in front of his friends that made her get some courage.

Mya walked up to them and yelled. "Really Kyle!"

Kyle stopped feeling on the girl on his lap as he looked up to a pissed off Mya.

"Who is this bitch?" the girl asked looking between Kyle and Mya.

"Watch your fucking mouth. This is my woman." Kyle said pushing the girl off his lap onto the floor.

Mya looked at Kyle and said "Right in my fucking face."

Getting up from the couch, he made a move to grab Mya as she tried to walk away from him.

"Get the fuck off of me Kyle." Mya said as she snatched her arm away from him.

"Baby she don't mean anything too me." Kyle said reaching to grab her again.

"Nigga you must think I'm dumb. You were all kissing on that bitch." Mya said mushing him upside the head.

"Mya, I know you upset but don't put your hands on me again." Kyle said forcefully.

"Nigga, whatever. You beat my ass all the time and I don't say shit." Mya said stepping up to his face.

"Bitch you must have really lost your mind. Don't let that liquor courage get you fucked up."

"Whatever. I'm ready to go." She said folding her arms across her chest.

"We ain't going anywhere."

"Well I'm leaving."

"How the fuck you plan on going anywhere with no fucking money huh? No fucking phone huh? Bitch go sit your ass down before you make me lose my cool in this bitch on my birthday." Kyle said angrily.

Mya knew she was stuck so she just went and sat down and drunk some more. Kyle told the girl to leave. He and Mya didn't say anything to each other for the rest of the night. She was drunk by the time the club was over with. When she went to stand up, she stumbled. Kyle looked at her with anger in his eyes while Natalia who was tipsy too, held her up.

"Come on momma, get it together." Natalia laughed.

"I love you so much Natalia." Mya slurred.

"I love you too sis."

Taye tapped Kyle.

"What?" Kyle asked when he turned to him.

"I know what you thinking. Don't do anything to that girl." Taye said with a somber expression on his face.

"Mind your fucking business." he said walking off towards Natalia and Mya.

Kyle grabbed Mya roughly and dragged her out of the club to the limo that awaited them. Once he opened the door, he threw her inside, causing her to hit her head against the other door.

"Ouch Kyle." Mya said, rubbing her forehead.

"What the fuck I tell you?" Kyle asked unbuttoning his shirt.

Before she could say anything, he punched her in the mouth, causing blood to fill it immediately. Kyle started to beat on Mya in the back of the limo car. After balling herself up, she got some courage and hit him back.

She refused to be the only one fucked up this time. The way they were fighting looked like the scene from "What's love got to do with it" with Ike and Tina Turner. The car stopped at their house, and Kyle grabbed her by her hair and dragged her out. Even though she fought back for the first time, she still got beat more when they made inside the house. The next morning they both woke up to bruises covering their bodies.

Chapter 7

Mya was finally healing up and needed to go to the grocery store. Kyle had taken all the keys in the house. When he leaves to go on trips or just to the hood he takes all the keys from her, leaving her to feel like a prisoner.

"Kyle, we have to go to the grocery store." Mya said

"Shit Mya." Kyle said while smoking his blunt.

"I can just drive to the store and come right back." Mya said shrugging.

"You must really like getting smacked."

She didn't even respond. She just got her purse and grocery list. Kyle walked out the door as Mya followed behind him. They pulled up at the Giant a short time later and got a cart. To anyone on the outside looking in, they looked like the perfect couple grocery shopping together.

"Babe I need some cheese." Mya said looking down at her list.

"I be back." He replied, walking off.

Mya was looking at the different steaks when she heard her name. She turned around and smiled when she saw who called her.

"Shad!" Shad had got finer. Taking in his 6'4, caramel complexion body, she noticed that his full pink lips were encased by a fully groomed goatee now. Looking up at his head, she saw that his hair was cut in deep waves. Making her way down his broad chest, she saw that his arms were full of tatts that led to a pair of big hands. Immediately Mya thought about what those hands would feel like on her. She shook her thoughts away when he started talking to her.

"Yes it's me baby." Shad said with his deep voice smiling down at Mya. He pulled her into a tight hug. She didn't miss the spark that was in his eyes when he saw her.

"You look good." Mya said stepping back to admire him. His shoulders were broad and the shirt he was wearing showed off the magnificent body underneath.

"Thank you. You look good as well."

Feeling self-conscious, she looked away and played in her hair. She thought she looked rough. She had on a baseball cap, loose sweats and a hoodie.

"You just being nice." Mya said biting her lip.

"Come on Mya. You know me."

Before Mya could respond, Kyle walked back over and looked Shad up and down, then laughed.

"Awwww man, Shad bitch ass. Thought you was in the country somewhere." Kyle said still laughing as he stood next to Mya.

"I'm visiting my people. Look, it was good seeing you again Mya." Shad said walking away before he beat the shit out of Kyle.

"Good seeing you too Shad." She replied in a low voice.

He smiled and walked off.

"Shad, you still trying I see." Kyle yelled after him.

Shad shook his head and kept walking. One day he knew Mya would come to her senses.

Kyle looked over to her and said "What was he doing in your face?"

"He called my name and just said hi." She replied.

"Yeah, whatever."

They finished shopping and went to the checkout line. Kyle's phone rang in his hand. Looking at the caller ID, he pulled out his wallet quickly. "Here, meet me at the car." He said giving her money before leaving.

Mya was putting the stuff on the belt and bent down to fast to pick up the sodas. She felt a sharp pain in her ribs from the beating a few days ago. A pair of hands picked the sodas up for her and put them on the belt.

"So where is your man?" Shad asked looking down at her. He saw the grimace cross her face when she tried to move.

"He had a call." She replied, not meeting his eyes.

"I can't believe you still with him. You can do so much better, Mya."

"I love him Shad. And better like who? You?" Mya asked looking at him.

"You love him but are you in love with him? I don't have to be the one Mya. I just want to see the girl I grew up with, the girl with the sparking hazel eyes, outgoing personality, and cheerful spirit." Shad said sincerely.

"Well, that little girl is long gone." she said, paying for her stuff and walking off.

"Mya, here." Shad said handing her one of her bags she forgot. Walking with the cart towards the car, she knew that Shad was watching her the whole way.

The whole ride back home, Mya was thinking about Shad's words and couldn't help but think how she lost so much of herself.

"Put the food up. I'll be back later. Make sure my dinner is ready too." Kyle said kissing her lips and then leaving out the house. Mya was putting the food up when a piece of paper fell out of the bag. She picked it up and started to read it.

Mya,

I didn't mean to upset you. I really do miss the old you. Hit me up sometime 202-555-8786.

Shad

She smiled at the note and went to hide it so Kyle wouldn't find it. After reading that note, it put her in a good mood. She made Kyle steak, mash potatoes, salad, and corn bread.

"Damn it smells good in here." Kyle said walking into the kitchen and kissing her on the cheek.

"Have a seat. I'll bring your plate to you."

Kyle sat down and Mya placed his plate in front of him. They both ate in silence while enjoying their meal.

"That was good as fuck baby." Kyle said wiping his mouth with his napkin.

"Thank you." Mya smiled, going to clean the kitchen up. She was washing the dishes when Kyle walked up behind her and started rubbing her ass. He turned her around and started kissing her. Pulling back, Mya looked at Kyle and started to picture him as Shad. She wrapped her arms around Kyle's neck and started to kiss him. He picked her up by her thighs and placed her on the counter. Pulling her sweats and underwear off, he unbuckled his jeans letting them drop to the floor; he grabbed his dick from out his boxers and stroked it up and down her slit, getting it wet. Mya used her legs and pulled Kyle into her, making his dick plunge into her. She was so wet from thinking about Shad being in Kyle's place. She wanted to moan his name so bad as she fucked him but she bit her lip to stop. Kyle didn't know what got into her but he liked it. Any other time they had sex, she would be quiet and let him get his nut off, but tonight she was fucking him back while moaning loudly. Getting lost in the thoughts of Shad again, she came hard. She knew then that it was serious because she rarely came when having sex with Kyle.

"Damn, that was great baby." Kyle said as he nutted in her. Pulling out, he grabbed a hand towel and wiped himself off.

Mya smiled and hopped off the counter. She made a move to go to the bathroom upstairs when Kyle stopped her.

"Where you going?" he asked.

"To take my shower." Mya said knowing the routine. After he got off, she would take a shower and come back to him to sleep.

"Not right now baby. We about to go again." He said smirking.

Mya looked at him in shock. After they finished round 2, they went upstairs and showered together. When they finished, they got into bed together. Kyle pulled her close to him and they cuddled. She didn't know what to make of his actions, but she loved the attention.

"I love you Mya."

"I love you too Kyle" she whispered as she drifted off to sleep.

Chapter 8

6 months later

"Wake that ass up! It's your fucking birthday." Kyle yelled to a still sleeping Mya.

She stretched her arms lazily above her head. Being able to see 19 was a great moment for her.

"Thank you." she said sitting up and seeing the food on the night stand that Kyle had prepared. Taking in the spread of eggs, bacon, grits and waffles, she smiled. The only time Kyle was extra nice and cooked was on her birthday.

"Look, today you and Natalia gonna go shopping, the spa, get your hair done and then you going out with your man tonight." Kyle said giving her the rundown of how she was spending her day.

"I can't wait." She said excitedly. It's been a month since Kyle put his hands on her, so she was feeling good.

"Well hurry up and eat. Taye said that Natalia would be here at 11."

Mya looked at the clock and noticed it was 9:30 am. After eating and showering, she put her hair in a bun, and threw on a sweater, jeans and boots. Natalia blew the horn from outside.

"See you later baby." Mya said giving Kyle a quick kiss.

Mya hopped in the car and was so happy to be with Natalia by herself and not with Kyle following her.

"So birthday girl, what you want to do?" Natalia asked as she drove off.

"I thought Kyle said I was going shopping, get my hair done and the spa." she said confused.

"Boo, I know your ass hasn't been away from that prison guard in God knows how long. I know it's something you want to do other than the shit he planned out for you." Natalia said.

"If I come home without my hair or shopping bags he will think something is up."

"I got this. Now tell me what you want to do? It's your day."

Mya thought for a minute and realized all her friends should be home for Christmas break.

"I want to see my friends." she said smiling. Just the thought of finally being able to see them after so long excited her.

"Well boo, we going to the south side."

Even though it was December, it was nice outside. It wasn't cold or hot. The temperature was perfect. Natalia pulled up around Mya old neighborhood and parked.

"There they go." Mya said spotting Destiny, Brittany, Tamara, and her sister friends Tiara, and Melanie.

"Well, what are we waiting for?" Natalia said getting out the car. Mya was nervous to see her friends after being away for so long. She walked up to them while they were sitting on the front of Destiny's building.

"Hey y'all." Mya said causing them to look up suddenly at the sound of her voice. Before she could blink, her friends had tackled her. They were all trying to hug her at the same time, while shouting questions at her.

"Mya, where the fuck you been at?" Brittany asked hugging her tightly.

"I have been around. I miss y'all." Mya said trying to hold her tears back. Just being surrounded by them again felt like she was truly home.

"We miss you too. We were just talking about you." Tamara said taking Mya in.

Mya raised an arched brow at Tamara. "Really?"

"Yea really bitch. Happy birthday." Destiny said hugging her again. "You thought we forgot what today was huh?"

"Thank you so much." Looking over to her right, she moved out the way to introduce her new friend. "Y'all this is my friend Natalia. Natalia this is Destiny, Tamara, Brittany, Tiara and Melanie."

Everyone made their own introductions.

Mya looked around her circle and asked, "So, what's new?"

"Shit the same. School is stressful as hell, but I love the A." Destiny said dancing around.

Mya was proud of her girls as they talked about college. She wished she was having the same experience as them. She looked down when she saw a little boy run over to Tamara. Raising her eyebrow again, she looked around at her friends. "Who had a baby?"

"That's my son." Tiara said, smiling down at her son as he pulled her leg for her to pick him up.

"You and Moss had a baby?" Mya asked surprised.

"Yea, and another one on the way." Tiara said rubbing her stomach.

Mya immediately thought of her sister. "Has my sister had any kids?"

Melanie and Tiara looked at each other. Melanie responded, "No she haven't."

She smiled and asked "Is she home?"

"Yea. She's on her way over here actually." Tiara said looking at her watch.

Mya smiled then bent down to Tiara and Moss son Mason. Putting her arms out and ran as fast as he could to her. Picking him up, she took in how adorable he was. Mason had long braids, light brown complexion, deep dimple on his left side, and some adorable soft brown eyes.

"Mason must like you Mya cause that bad nigga don't go to anyone." Brittany said laughing.

Everyone was talking and enjoying hanging out. Natalia fit right in with them as she was laughing with Melanie while they were talking.

Laurel walked up to them texting on her phone. She didn't even take in that Mya was standing with her friends.

"Why you look like that?" Tiara asked Laurel. Her face was screwed up as she held her phone in a death grip.

"This nigga is blowing me. I just get home and he acting like a bitch. Swear he must be having his period." Laurel said causing everyone to laugh. When she finally looked up from her phone, it was to see her sister. Her face dropped as tears started to fall down her cheeks. Mya stood up as Laurel walked to her. They both reached for each other at the same time, hugging tightly.

"Mya, I've missed you. Happy birthday." Laurel said not wanting to let her little sister go.

"I've missed you too and thank you." Mya said looking at her sister. "You look great. Getting thick I see. Got Loyalty putting it on you?"

"Shut up." Laurel said laughing and hugging her again.

"Aww ain't this so fucking cute." Lord said walking up behind them holding Keya's hand.

Laurel and Mya looked at Lord and smiled.

"Lord." Mya said running up to him and giving him a side hug. She missed him so much.

"What's up little sis? Happy birthday." Lord said. He missed seeing Mya around.

"Thank you. What's up with you though? I see you finally got with Keya." She looked over at Keya and said "I told him way back y'all need to make it official."

"He should have listened to you." Keya said laughing.

"Yea yea. I'm with her now that's all that matters." Lord said.

Mya was having such a good time with her sister and friends that she didn't want to leave. Natalia reached into her bag when she felt her phone vibrating. Looking at the text message on her screen, she looked over to Mya.

"That was Taye, Mya. We still have to get your hair done."

Mya took a deep breath and looked at her friends and sister. Giving them a faint smile, she said "I love all you guys. I'll see y'all later." Mya said hugging all of them, kissing Mason on the cheek, and when she got to Laurel she held her tight. "I'm fine, Laurel." she said kissing her sister on the cheek.

Laurel let her go and looked on as Mya walked off.

Mya and Natalia were walking to the car when she saw her mother. She took off running to and hugged her, taking Liz by surprise.

"I love you mommy." Mya said hugging her mother tight. She missed her mother so much. Laurel was watching the interaction between her mother and sister and walked up to them. Liz missed her children and talking to Loyalty made her realizes how wrong she had been to them. All three of them were hugging and crying. Their friends watched on in amazement that Liz was embracing her two daughters.

"I love you both." Liz said, her voice cracking slightly from her emotions.

"Mya we have to go." Natalia said not wanting to interrupt their moment but she didn't want Mya to get in trouble with Kyle for being home late.

Mya smiled at her mother and sister as she let them go and backed away. She was walking away when she heard her mother's voice.

"Happy birthday baby." Liz said smiling at her and blowing her a kiss.

"Thank you mommy." Mya said, blowing a kiss back and getting in the car. She cried all the way to the salon. After getting her hair done, she stayed quiet throughout the rest of the day as they did the things Kyle planned.

Natalia pulled up to Mya's house and looked at her. "Are you ok?" she asked.

Mya looked at Natalia. She smiled and hugged her. "I'm great. Thank you so much. You made this a great birthday."

"That's what friends are for." Natalia said as she hugged her back.

Mya got out the car, got her bags and headed in the house. As soon as she stepped through the door, she was hit in the face.

"Mya I tried to be nice to you cause it was your birthday, but you tried to be slick." Kyle said punching her again. "I told you to go shopping, the spa, and get your fucking hair done. But your ass went around your old way. Now I have to teach your ass a lesson on your birthday for disrespecting me. Then you were around that nigga Lord."

Kyle beat Mya till she was unconscious and not moving. He kneeled down and put his hand under her nose. Seeing that she was still breathing, he took a deep breath and picked her up. Putting her in their bed after cleaning the blood off her face, he put his shoes on and left her in the house.

Chapter 9

Kyle

After Kyle beat Mya unconscious, he went to his side chick, Ashley house. Knocking on the door, Ashley opened it, holding their 1 year old daughter on her hip.

"What you doing here? I thought you would be with your wifey. It's her birthday right? All them damn post on Facebook you put up." Ashley said catching a attitude.

"Chill with that shit. Let me see my daughter." Kyle said taking his daughter Kyla from her.

Kyle wasn't worried about Mya finding out about his daughter because he controlled everything she did. Even though Kyle didn't want any kids, he loves his daughter. He sometimes wondered what his kids with Mya would have looked like. Pushing the thought from his head, he played with Kyla in his arms.

"For real, what are you doing here Kyle?" Ashley asked.

"I just wanted to come over and chill. Damn is that a problem?" Kyle asked getting pissed off. Ashley had never seen the abusive side of him.

"Umm hmm." Ashley said.

Kyle rocked his daughter to sleep and laid her in her crib. He came back and pulled Ashley on his lap as he sat on the couch.

"You going to give daddy some pussy?" Kyle asked rubbing her through her pants.

"What about your wife?" Ashley moaned out.

"I'm here with you right now. Why you keep asking about her for?" Kyle asked getting angry.

"No reason."

"Man give me some head."

Ashley wasted no time getting between his legs and giving him head. Showing no respect for her, he begins to roughly thrust himself in and out of her mouth. Pulling her up, he bent her over the couch, pulling her pants down and entering her roughly. He was in the middle of fucking Ashley over the side of the couch, when his phone rang. Before he got to Ashley's house, he wanted to end Lord's life, just because he didn't like him as much as he didn't like Loyalty and Shad. He told his workers to let him know if they see him.

"Yo." Kyle said pounding into Ashley.

"He around your girl way." Pete said.

"Cool. I'll be around the way in a little." Kyle said hanging up.

Kyle pumped faster till he came inside of Ashley. Pulling his pants up, he made his way to the door.

"Where you going?" Ashley asked, still bent over the couch.

"I have shit to do." Kyle said leaving out, not giving her a glance. He pulled up to his trap house and got out. "Let's do this." he said talking to Slim and Pete. He didn't let Taye know what the plan was. He felt like he was becoming too soft lately. They got in a tinted out car, drinking and passing a blunt the whole way to Mya's old neighborhood.

"Nigga, why you after that nigga Lord? He going to the NBA soon." Pete asked hitting the blunt from the passenger seat.

"The only place that nigga going is to the grave. Fuck you mean." Kyle said from the back loading his gun.

—*—*—

Laurel …

"I'm about to take him in my mother house. Be right back." Tiara said picking Mason up.

"Hurry up cause I'm about to leave. Loyalty calling me." Laurel said looking down at her phone. She had just finished talking with her mom and told her she would stop by a little later.

"Tell him you gonna give him some." Tiara laughed over her shoulder as she walked upstairs.

"Baby, you staying at my house?" Keya asked Lord.

"Naw I'm gonna go home. I have to see my momma woman." Lord said leaning down to kiss her fully on the lips.

"Nigga what the fuck is up." Cash said giving Lord a manly hug as he walked up from the other side of the street.

"Ain't shit nigga." Lord said dapping him up.

Cash looked at Laurel and said "What's up baby? I've missed you."

"Bye Cash. I don't have time for you." Laurel said not paying any attention to him.

"Same ole Laurel. You talk to Mike?" Cash asked changing the subject.

"Yea, he good."

"Tell him I got his books soon."

"I will."

It was a weird feeling that everyone felt at the same time. Everything and everyone had got quiet.

"Something ain't right." As soon as the words left Lord's mouth, bullets started flying in their direction. Everyone was ducking and running. Mike's boys pulled out their guns and started shooting back at the tinted car as it sped past. Cash pulled Laurel down as a bullet missed her head by an inch. Lord grabbed Keya and shielded her. As soon as it started, it stopped as the car sped off down the street.

Keya started to scream "Call an ambulance." Lord had rolled off of her and she saw the blood coming from his chest. "Please baby, stay with me." Keya said putting pressure on the wounds.

"I'm good. Just tell them to hurry up." Lord said weakly.

"They on their way Keya." Destiny said helping Keya out by checking his pulse.

Lord looked at Destiny and Keya and said "My two doctors."

"Just keep the jokes coming Lord until the paramedics get here." Destiny said, giving him a watery smile.

When the paramedics got there, they loaded Lord onto the back immediately. His cousin Heaven had gone to get his mother after she came outside and saw the commotion.

Laurel's phone rang at that moment. Not even looking at the screen, she answered in a shaky voice, "Hello."

"What's wrong?" Loyalty asked, knowing something was wrong off jump.

"It was just a drive by around the way. I'm shaken up a little."

"A drive by." Loyalty said causing Moss and Kelly to look at him.

"Yes. Baby it happened so suddenly." She said, still trying to wrap her head around it.

"Is everyone ok?" Loyalty asked getting in the car with Moss and Kelly.

"Lord was shot. He was rushed to the hospital. All the girls are fine." Laurel was so happy her mother went to work so she didn't have to worry about her being in the crossfire.

"I'm on my way. Don't try and drive."

"Ok." Laurel said hanging up.

Laurel looked at Keya and Destiny who were covered in Lord's blood. Lord's mother had run out of her building and straight for the ambulance. As soon as she was in the back, the truck pulled off.

"Keya, let's go." Heaven yelled coming out the building.

Keya looked at Destiny and asked "Are you coming?"

"I will be up there in a few. I have to check on my mom and them."

"Ok." Keya gave her a hug and ran to Heaven's car.

Laurel pulled Destiny into a hug.

"I hope he is ok. He's our big brother." Destiny cried onto her shoulder.

"I'm sure he is going to be fine." Laurel said rubbing her back.

"I'm going to go check on my family." Destiny said wiping her eyes. Turning around, she walked into her mother's building.

Everyone else decided to go to Tiara's house. 20 minutes later, there was a knock on the door.

"Who is it?" Tamara asked as she walked to the door.

"Me." MOss said from the other side.

Tamara opened the door and let Moss, Kelly and Loyalty in.

"Where is Mason?" Moss asked Tiara as he pulled her into a hug.

"He in the room with my mother." She said, breathing in his clean scent.

Moss took a breath of relief. If anything would have happened to his little man, he was gonna tear the whole neighborhood apart.

"Did anyone get a look at who was shooting?" Loyalty asked as he sat next to Laurel. Her head was on his chest as he stroked her hair.

Everyone shook their head no. Before any more questions were asked, there was another knock at the door.

"Who is it?" Tamara asked.

"It's Cash."

Tamara opened the door and let him in. He looked at Loyalty, Moss and Kelly, mugging them.

"I just wanted to make sure all of y'all were good. I'm letting you know we will find out who did that bamma shit." Cash said as he looked to Laurel.

"We good Cash and thank you." Laurel said, sitting up straight.

"It's no problem." Cash said leaving out after saying bye to the girls.

Loyalty looked at Laurel. Getting up from the couch, he pulled Laurel up. Saying goodnight, they walked to her car and got in.

"What you thank him for?" Loyalty asked as soon as he closed the car door.

"He saved my life. He pulled me down when a bullet was inches away from my head."

"Baby are you ok?" Loyalty asked, feeling bad for not checking her out.

"I was so scared. I saw my life flash before my eyes." Laurel said, looking straight ahead in the car. The shooting kept playing through her mind. Loyalty didn't care that he was driving. He pulled over on the side of the road and pulled Laurel across the seat to him. Kissing her forehead, he whispered in her ear how much he loved her. He vowed to her that whoever the shooter was, they would pay.

Chapter 10

Mya.....

Mya woke up weak and with a headache that was pounding. She tried to remember what happened. The last thing she remembered was it being her birthday and seeing her family and friends. She stood up to go to the bathroom and collapsed on the floor. Right at that moment, Kyle walked into the room with a blunt to his lips.

"You aight?" Kyle asked.

"My body is in so much pain." Mya said, remembering the ass whipping he put on her.

Kyle picked her up and took her to the bathroom. He was starting to get a little worried about her. She had been unconscious for three days straight. He kept making sure she was breathing though. While she used the bathroom, he ran her some hot bath water.

"What day is it?" Mya asked, squinting against the light from the vanity.

"It's the 18th." Kyle said like it was nothing.

Mya looked at him like he was crazy. She couldn't believe that he beat her into a coma.

"I'm sorry for hitting you Mya like that." Kyle said putting her in the tub after she took her clothes off.

Mya didn't say anything. She knew by now that he was only trying to save face. Kyle left her to relax in the tub and went to fix her something to eat. When she was done relaxing, she got up and took a shower. Her body was still in pain, so she cut her shower short. After changing up, she went into the room and turned the news on. Taking a close look, she saw her neighborhood on the screen and turned the volume up.

"Latest news on the shooting that happened three days ago around Hill Towers, leaving three people seriously injured. Stephanie Folks, Frank Wells, and Lord Mitchell are still in critical condition. So far there are no leads on who the shooter is or the motive."

She put her hand over her mouth and gasped, "Oh my God."

Kyle walked in and looked at what was playing on the TV. "I see you heard about your friend."

"Who would shoot Lord? He wasn't involved in anything. Stephanie was my next door neighbor. She had the biggest crush on Mike." Mya said still trying to comprehend who would hurt them.

Kyle didn't say anything to that. "Here is your food." he said handing her some soup.

Mya ate the food and drank some water. After she ate, she laid back down and went to sleep.

1 week later…

It was now Christmas and Mya was slowly healing. She hadn't been out the house since her birthday. She and Kyle planned on having Christmas dinner together and opening gifts. The doorbell rang just as she was taking the turkey out of the oven. She wasn't expecting anyone so she just shrugged and walked to the door.

"Who is it?" Mya asked as she got closer.

"Ashley."

Opening the door, she came face to face with a girl that she had never seen before.

"Yes." Mya asked noticing the baby she was holding on her hip.

"Since Kyle don't like to answer his phone, I figure I would bring his daughter to him on Christmas." Ashley said.

"He not here." Mya said looking at the baby girl she was holding.

"Well, you her stepmother. Watch her." Ashley said handing her the baby.

Mya took Kyla from Ashley along with her bag and car seat.

"Oh and her name is Kyla." Ashley said walking away and heading to her car.

Mya closed the door and looked at the baby, wanting to cry. She was the spitting image of Kyle.

"That bastard." she said, taking the baby's coat off and putting her in the car seat while she finished cooking. When she was done, she called Kyle over and over. It was now 10pm and he was supposed to have been home at 4. Not wanting to waste the food, Kyla and Mya ate dinner together. Mya fed her mashed potatoes and cranberry sauce with little pieces of turkey. After they finished, she took Kyla to the couch to rest. They were both sleep, with Kyla on her chest, when Kyle walked in the house. When he walked into the living room, he almost passed out after seeing Kyla laying on Mya's chest.

"Mya." he said, waking her up.

Mya opened her eyes and looked at him.

"What is she doing here?" Kyle asked pointing to Kyla.

"Kyle just go and put her in the bed please." Mya said, closing her eyes again.

Kyle picked her up and took her to their room. Putting her in the middle of their bed, he placed pillows around her. When he went back downstairs, Mya had fixed his plate.

"Baby, let me explain." Kyle said moving to grab her.

"Explain what Kyle! That you had a baby on me. That Ashley was good enough to carry your child, but every fucking time I got pregnant, you beat it out of me." Mya said with tears running down her face. To actually see evidence of Kyle's betrayal broke Mya once and for all.

"No, it's not like that." Kyle said pulling her into a hug.

"Kyle you always say you love me, but you continually doing me wrong. You beat my ass, you kill our babies, you fuck a chick and get her pregnant, and you come home smelling like a bitch. It's fucking Christmas and I'm the woman you suppose to love but I have to spend it alone while you out fucking who knows. Maybe another baby momma. You don't love me Kyle." Mya said with a stern voice.

"I do love you, Mya. Don't ever say that. You my world baby. Those other bitches don't mean anything to me." Kyle said, trying to plead with her.

"Sure you do." She said, walking away from him. She went upstairs and got in the bed with Kyla.

Mya and Kyle had Kyla for a week before Ashley started blowing his phone up, telling him to bring her daughter to her. It was New Year's Eve.

"Baby I'm going to take Kyla home and when I come back we are going to head to the party." Kyle said holding the baby in his arms.

Mya didn't say anything. She leaned over and gave Kyla a kiss on the cheek. Ever since she found out about Kyla, she hadn't been talking to Kyle. He just figured she was still pissed with him.

When Kyle left, Mya looked in her closet at all her clothes. She stopped at dress that she always loved but never got a chance to wear. Pulling it out, she found the perfect shoes to match, along with accessories. Looking at the clock, it read 10 pm. When Kyle walked back in the house, she knew he had just finished having sex with Ashley because he went straight to the shower. He had already taken a shower right before he went to take Kyla home.

"Baby you know what you wearing?" Kyle asked once he got out the shower.

"I'm not going." She said, looking uninterested.

"What you mean? It's New year's Eve." Kyle said giving her a crazy look.

"I'm not feeling well." She lied.

"Whatever."

Kyle got dressed and looked at her. "Happy New Year."

Mya didn't say anything back to him. He sighed and walked out the house.

Mya took a shower and put the dress on that she laid out earlier. She flat ironed her hair, put her shoes on and did her make up. She looked in the mirror and smiled at how she looked. She knew that when she was found, she would still look pretty. Sitting at her desk, she pulled out paper and a pen and began to write. She wrote to a total of eleven people, explaining her actions to come. When she looked at the clocked, she noticed it was almost time for the count down. She grabbed her bottles she stashed and started her New Year's party. Grabbing her phone, she sent a text to Destiny and Natalia.

Chapter 11

Destiny…

After Lord got shot, Destiny stayed in the house. She went and checked up on him frequently. He would always tell her the same thing each time.

"I'm good sis. You don't have to keep worrying about me."

Since today was New Year's Eve, Scott asked Destiny to come to a party with him. Even though she didn't want to go, she wanted to spend some time with him since they barely saw each other while being home.

When they arrived to the party, they were greeted by all their friends. After making their rounds and dancing, the countdown started.

"10, 9, 8, 7, 6, 5, 4,3,2,1… Happy new year's." was yelled across the party.

"Happy New Year's baby." Scott said kissing her.

Destiny was about to respond when someone tapped her on the shoulder.

"I knew that was you. How you been? I heard about Lord." Natalia said as she gave Destiny a hug.

"I've been making it." Before Destiny could respond further, she and Natalia text message ringer went off at the same time, showing Mya's name. They read their messages at the same time, not realizing that they were reading them out loud.

"Destiny I love you and thank you for always being in my life. I'll never forget the memories as I hope you will always remember me. "

"Natalia, thank you for being a great friend to me. Till we meet again. I love you!"

Destiny and Natalia looked at each other, putting the pieces together that Mya was saying good bye.

"We have to get to Mya and fast." Natalia said frantically.

"I don't know where she lives." Destiny said, her eyes clouding with unshed tears. If anything happened to her best friend, she wouldn't know how to take it.

"I do. Let's go." Natalia said making her way to the exit.

"Scott we have to go. Something is wrong with Mya." Destiny said pulling his hand through the crowd.

"Let's go." Scott said without asking a question.

Natalia went and found Taye, and the four of them ran to Taye's truck and headed to Mya and Kyle's house.

They kept calling Mya's phone but it was going straight to voicemail. Pulling up to the house, Destiny didn't give the car enough time to stop. She was banging on the door, but got no answer.

"Des, I got it." Taye said kicking the door down.

Natalia and Destiny ran upstairs to Mya's room. They saw her lying on the bed, dressed up. She looked as if she was sleep, but the 5 empty pill bottles and two empty vodka bottles told a different story.

"Oh my God. Please don't die Mya." Destiny said checking her pulse noticing how faint it was, she knew she had to get some of the pills out of her system. Without a second thought Destiny, put her finger down Mya's throat making her throw up some of the pills. Tears were streaming down her face as she held Mya's head in her lap. "Natalia, she still has a pulse. We need to get her to the hospital right now. We don't have time to wait for the paramedics. We have to get her there now. Can you guys pick her up please?" Destiny asked Scott and Taye, after checking her pulse again. It wasn't as faint as before.

Taye and Scott wasted no time picking her up. Natalia picked something up off the desk in the room and they all ran out the house, heading to the hospital. Destiny was talking to Mya the whole way while holding her head in her lap.

"I need to call Kyle." Taye said from the front seat.

"No!" Destiny and Natalia said at the same time.

"Baby don't you call him. He is the reason why she tried to commit suicide." Natalia said.

Taye looked at Natalia and saw the tears in her eyes. He knew the right thing to do would be to leave Kyle out of this. Looking at both Destiny and Natalia, he said, "Ok."

When they pulled up to the entrance to the hospital, Scott jumped out and ran inside. 20 seconds later, he returned with a few nurses and doctors and a bed. They transported Mya from the car to the bed, immediately leaving and heading inside.

Destiny picked up her phone and dialed Laurel's number as she went into the waiting room.

"Hello." Laurel answered with a lot of music in the background.

"Laurel, come to Ft. Washington Hospital." Destiny said.

"What for?" Laurel asked. Her background had gotten quiet, so she knew Laurel stepped out of where she was.

"Mya tried to commit suicide." Destiny said. The line went dead as soon as she finished her sentence. She looked at her phone and saw that Laurel had hung up. Getting ready to call her back, Destiny's phone rang instead.

"Hello." Destiny answered.

"What is going on Destiny?" Loyalty yelled. Destiny could hear Laurel in the background screaming.

"Mya tried to commit suicide. We at Ft. Washington Hospital." Destiny said.

"We on our way." Loyalty said hanging up.

Destiny texted her mom and told her where she was. Her mother said she was going to go let Liz know. Destiny looked over at Natalia and saw she was crying reading what looked like a letter.

"What you reading?" Destiny asked as she moved closer to her.

Before Natalia could respond, the waiting room filled up with people for Mya. Even Liz was there with her work attire on.

"What is going on?" Liz asked Destiny frantically.

"Mrs. Adams, me and Natalia" she started, pointing to her, "got a text from Mya. It was like a good bye text, so we knew something wasn't right. We hurried to her house and she had taken a lot of pills and liquor. We have to wait on word from the doctors, but they said they were going to pump her stomach."

"Oh my God, thank you for getting her here." Liz said placing her hand over her mouth and crying. Laurel came up beside her mother and hugged her.

"Read that letter, Natalia." Destiny said. Everyone was gathered around, as Natalia began to read the first line:

I'm writing this letter because I can't take life anymore. Everyone that I mention in this letter impacted my life in some way shape or form. If I forgot you, please don't take it to heart. I'm racing against time.

Dear Mom and Dad,

I love you both. Even though we had our ups and down, I wouldn't ask for anyone else as my parents. Ma, growing up, I used to say I will never be like you, because I always witnessed daddy abusing you. Dad, I always said I would never date anyone like you: a man who beat women for fun. But I guess I'm just like the both of you. I'm dating a man just like my father. I see why you were so relieved when daddy got locked up. On a lighter note, I don't have to worry about that anymore. I just want to say I love you both.

Dear Mikey,

I love you big bro. You are still my rock. You were my brother and father, and I appreciate everything you've done for me. I'm okay Mike. Don't worry about me. I love you.

Dear Laurel and Loyalty,

Words can't explain how much I appreciate you two. Laurel you are the woman I want to grow up to be like. You're smart, you're beautiful and you're just an all around boss bitch. You walk in a room and all the attention goes to you and you don't even try. I should have listened to you all those times you tried to warn me and tell me don't go back to him, but I was so lost and in love, that I didn't want to listen to anyone until it was too late. I'm sorry. I know you probably crying like a little baby with your emotional self, but at least you have a man like Loyalty who will hold you down. Loyalty, thank you for being in my sister's life. Thank you for being a great big brother to me. Oh and thank you for beating the shit out of Kyle that time. I laugh every time I think about it. I love you both so much.

Dear Destiny and Scott

You have been my best friend, my sister, ace since I can remember. Thank you! Even when we fuss and fight, we could never stay mad at each other. I should have listened to you, but like you said I'm just hard headed. Shoot, I couldn't see my life without you in it. I brought a cell phone just so I can keep in contact with you. Nothing was going to stop our bond. So don't let this stop our bond either. I love you. Scott, Thank you for making Destiny happy, loving her and treating her right. I also want to thank you for always sticking up for me. I love you too.

Dear Brittany and Tamara

We all we got. I'm so proud of y'all and when I saw y'all for my birthday and y'all were telling me about the college life ,all I could do was wish I was there with you guys. I'm so glad that we became friends. I love y'all! Walk across those stages for me.

Dear Lord,

You started off as my crush, and ended up as my best friend/ big brother. I'm so happy you're finally with Keya by time nigga. I'm also sorry that you got shot. I feel like it's my fault because I really think that dumb ass Kyle did it. When I found out you was shot, I saw a smirk on his face. I love you and I'm finally away.

Dear Natalia and Taye

Thank you two so much. Natalia you became like a sister to me, helping me out any way you could. When I was lonely, you were there for me. Words can't express how much that meant to me. I love you for that. Taye I was always so happy when you were around the house because I didn't have to fear him. I knew you wouldn't let him hurt me in front of you. Who would have thought when I first met you I thought you was a creep. Thank you so much for being there.

Dear Shad,

You don't understand how much your words meant to me when you saw me at the Giant. I always saw the spark in your eyes towards me, but I didn't know how to respond to it. Anytime I needed you, you were there no questions asked. I knew when you told me that I need to find the right man that you were talking about yourself. And you were right. Even when you were at the hospital with me you would not leaving my side. I don't know why I didn't see it then, but I'm letting you know now that I always did love you Shad.

Dear Kyle,

I don't know where to start. You hurt me so bad that I hate you. I wish you would die a slow death. You beat me, belittled me, broke me, made me feel unworthy, un-loved, and depressed. Before I met you I was happy, then you changed all of that. You used my mind and eagerness and the loved I had for you to your benefit and took advantage of me. Don't get me wrong, it wasn't all bad. There were some good days, but the bad outweighed them. My last straw was you beating my ass on my birthday and I was out of it for three fucking days. Then on Christmas day I find out you had a daughter, by a chick you claim is your friend. I dealt with ass whippings over dumb shit; I dealt with the women, the cheating, but having a baby on me, broke my soul. I can't blame you for everything, because I became a weak minded woman who let a man dictate her life and that was my fault. But the rest is on you. I'm so happy to finally escape you. You ain't shit just like your father. Karma will be with you soon.

I know I'm missing some people but it's time to count down, I love you all. Live your life and do not cry over me. I'm finally at peace.

Love

Mya Adams

After Natalia finished reading the letter, there wasn't a dry eye in the room.

"I'm going to kill that nigga." Shad said wiping his eyes. He didn't care that he was crying. The girl he loved was fighting for her life at that moment.

"Calm down Shad." Melanie said, putting a hand on her cousin's shoulder.

"He was beating her ass. I had a feeling he was but no proof. Melanie you know how I feel about her. Let anything happen to her, I'm bodying him." Shad said getting angry now.

"Cuz just chill out. You letting your emotions get in the way." Kelly said trying to keep him calm.

Loyalty was sitting there holding Laurel while she cried thinking of ways he was going to kill Kyle.

"Family of Mya Adams." The doctor said as he walked in with a clipboard in his hand.

They stood up. Liz walked ahead of everyone and stood before the doctor.

"I'm Dr. Smith. Ms. Adams took a large amount of sleeping and pain pills and consumed a large amount of alcohol. We had to pump her stomach twice to ensure that everything was out. She also had bruising around her rib area. We tested to make sure she didn't have any internal bleeding. She will be here for a while so we can monitor her recovery and keep an eye on the bruising on her ribs."

"May we see her?" Liz asked anxiously.

"Ma'am, it's a lot of family here and she really needs to rest." Dr. Smith explained.

"Look, how about you let my mother-in-law and wife go see her. The rest of us will wait." Loyalty said.

"That's fine." Dr. Smith said escorting Liz and Laurel to Mya's room.

When they went inside, Mya was sleeping peacefully with the monitor beeping. She had so many tubes connected to her, but Liz rather see that, than her daughter in a casket.

"We're here for you baby." Liz said kissing Mya's forehead.

"We love you Mya. Get some rest baby girl. We'll be back in the morning." Laurel said kissing her cheek.

Liz and Laurel went back downstairs to update everyone on how Mya was doing.

"I will see you all tomorrow." Liz said after she hugged her daughter and their friends. She had a lot to think about, starting with repairing her relationship with her children.

"Call me when you get home ma." Laurel said hugging her back and kissing her cheek.

"Ok." she said, waving as she left.

"She's not going back to him. I don't even want him to know where she is." Laurel said.

"We need to go get her things." Destiny chimed in.

Taye stepped forward. "Look, Kyle is my best friend but I always checked him how he was treating Mya. Y'all can go by the house and get her stuff now. That nigga still clubbing and he is going to this chick house afterwards. But if y'all move her, she can't stay with you Loyalty. He will find her. Whether Mya want to admit it or not, if he charms her, she will be back with him. So she will have to leave DC for a while."

"Taye is right." Loyalty spoke up.

"She can move with me down Charlotte. I'm going into my junior year of college and I have an apartment down there." Shad said

"I don't know how I feel about my sister moving in with a guy again." Laurel said, skeptical of the situation.

"Laurel, you've known me since forever. I won't do anything to hurt her." he said. Laurel knew it was true. Besides Lord, she trusted Shad with Mya.

"She can move to Atlanta with me and Scott also." Destiny threw out.

"How about we let Mya pick when she wakes up. Right now let's go get her shit and pray that nigga there so I can handle him." Moss said, itching to lay hands on Kyle.

Everyone left and headed to Kyle's house. When they got there, the door was still opened, so they knew he wasn't home. They grabbed her stuff from the bedroom and started packing. She had pictures hidden of her family, friends and everything. After the girls finished, they had a total of 10 bags. They left and didn't look back, still leaving the door wide open.

Chapter 12

Mya...

It had been a week and there wasn't any sign of her waking up. Everyday someone was there visiting her. Shad told the nurses that Mya was his fiancé so he could spend the night with her. He just wanted to make sure that Kyle didn't find her and Liz agreed to him staying with her.

Today wasn't any different. Shad was sleep in the chair next to Mya's bed, when the nurse came in.

"Good morning." The nurse said to Shad when she noticed he was waking up.

"Good morning. How is she doing?" Shad asked stretching.

"Her vitals are good. Her organs are good. She's just in a deep state of sleep. She will wake up soon." The nurse said smiling at him.

"I hope she does. I miss her." He replied, looking her over.

"I'm sure she misses you too." The nurse said as she finished up and left out.

Shad laid his head back and thought about what he was going to do. He had to go back to school soon but he didn't want to leave Mya. He needed her to wake.

"Lord, I come to you again to ask that you wake Mya from her sleep and protect her. Let her know that her family and friends are all waiting to see and talk to her. In your name Jesus I pray. Amen." Shad said, ending his prayer.

Mya opened her eyes as soon as he finished praying and looked at the white light above her. "I hope I'm in heaven." She thought to herself. Attempting to move, her body was wracked with pain.

"Mya, baby don't move. I'm going to get the nurse." Shad said, leaving the room and going to the nurse's station.

As soon as Mya laid her head back against the pillows, a team of nurses and doctors came. They started flashing lights in her eyes, checking her out. A nurse helped remove her feeding tube as the others looked on.

"How are you feeling Mya?" Dr. Smith asked as he reviewed her vitals.

"Thirsty." Mya said weakly, her throat raw.

"That's understandable." Dr. Smith said giving her some water to sip from.

"I will be back to check on you in a bit." Dr. Smith said. "Try and relax. Don't talk so much. Try and use pen and paper if you need to communicate.

"Ok."

Everyone left out leaving her and Shad alone. She finally looked over at the chair he was sitting in and smiled.

"I'm glad you're woke." Shad said, smiling at her.

Mya looked down ashamed of what she did. She was even more ashamed she tried to kill herself and now had to face the people she loved. She knew they had to have read the letter she left behind.

"What are you doing here?" Mya asked.

"I've been here ever since Destiny and Natalia brought you here. I haven't left your side Mya. I love you." Shad said getting up and looking her in the eyes as he walked to her.

"No you don't." Mya said not understanding how he could love her. Not after the fool she made of herself.

Caressing the side of her face, Shad moved her cheek till her eyes were looking at him. "Mya I've been loved you. Me almost losing you made me know that I can't live another day without you."

Before Mya could respond, the door to her room opened. Her friends and family piled in, one after the other. Shad had sent a mass text out letting them know Mya was finally woke. Laurel and Liz ran to the bed showering her with kisses.

"Ma, Laurel really." Mya said frowning.

"Y'all gotta let baby girl breathe Ma." Loyalty laughed from behind them.

Mya looked at him with an eyebrow raised when he called her mother ma. That was the first time she had heard him make that reference.

"Aww my baby is finally up. Lawdddddd yesss she is up." Kelly said in a fake high pitched voice. He was walking in the room with Melanie, Moss, Tiara, Mason, Tamara, Micah, Brittany, Eric, Scott and Destiny. They all had balloons, flowers, bears and candy. Mya's room was more decorated than the gift shop downstairs. Everyone took turns giving Mya a hug.

"Don't you ever do that to me ever again May. You scared the shit out of me. Excuse my language Mrs. Adams. But for real, I was scared." Destiny said while holding her hand.

"I'm sorry. I didn't mean to scare you Destiny, or any of you. I just thought that ending my life was the right thing to do. I had caused so much stress and heartache to some of you. My life was just in shambles. I just didn't wanna be here anymore."

"You should have just came to us." Laurel said grasping her hand. "We all would have helped you in any way we could. Ending your life was not the solution. You know that every person in this room cares about and loves you more than anything."

"Yea sis. I told you plenty of times to come home." Loyalty said. "We would have took care of you and helped you out."

"I know but... never mind. I'm sorry for what I did." Mya said taking a deep breath. "I promise to never let it get this far or this bad ever again."

"Enough of the past. Let her live right now." Shad said smiling over at her.

Mya looked at him and gave him a smile.

"Um does Kyle know where I am?" Mya asked looking around the room at everyone.

"Look, we decided to not tell him where you at." Scott said.

Mya breathed a sigh of relief and said "Thank you." She was feeling a little overwhelmed and wanted to rest.

"How about all of you leave and let Mya get some rest?" Liz said noticing that her eyes were starting to droop a little.

Everyone gave Mya a hug and left. Destiny, Scott, Shad, Liz, Loyalty and Laurel stayed behind.

"We've been talking" Destiny started, gesturing to everyone around the room, "and we think that it would be better if you leave DC for a while. We're not sure what Kyle is capable off since you've been gone for a week."

"And where am I supposed to go?" Mya asked a little afraid.

"You can come to Boston with me, go to ATL with Destiny and Scott or you can go with Shad to Charlotte." Laurel said, naming the places to go.

"Can I think about it? I know all of you have to get back to school and I don't want to be a burden on any of you." Mya said wringing her hands together.

"You're not a burden. We want to make sure you're safe." Shad said.

Mya smiled at them then laid back against the pillows. Next thing she knew she was sleep again.

—*—*—

Kyle...

A week after New Year's Day is when he finally returned home, Kyle was walking back and forth wondering who the fuck had the nerve to break down his door. He was also wondering where the fuck Mya was at. He called every hospital, police station and had some of his boys looking for her with no luck.

He picked up his phone and called Taye.

"Hello." Taye answered in his sleep voice. He looked at the clock and saw it was 4am.

"Nigga wake the fuck up! Call the crew! We have an emergency." Kyle yelled into the phone.

"What type of emergency at 4am?" Taye asked still half sleep.

Still yelling, he replied, "I fucking come home and my fuckin door is kicked in, shit missing and I can't find Mya ass anywhere."

"Wait, it wasn't like that yesterday?" Taye asked confused. He knew they kicked the door in a week ago. He should have been aware of that before then.

"Man, I knew Mya was mad and tripping and shit so I was over Ashley house to let her cool off, but when I get here this is what I fucking see." Kyle explained.

"Aight. Imma call the niggas." Taye said ready to go back to sleep.

"Yeah do that." Kyle said hanging up. He finally looked at the closet, the dresser drawers, the bathroom and realized that the only shit missing was Mya's.

"What the fuck? I know that bitch didn't do what I think she did. Naw she not stupid. That bitch couldn't leave me. She don't have anyone." He said, talking to himself. Taking the bottle of Remy from the kitchen counter, he started to drink. He took another sip of the liquor and thought about her behavior recently. "She wasn't doing rebellious shit until she started hanging out with Taye bitch. Oh ok, she got my woman to leave me. Ok I might have to kill that bitch after I find Mya." Picking up his phone, he dialed Taye's house number.

"Hello." A groggily Natalia answered.

"Bitch where the fuck is Mya?" Kyle yelled in the phone.

Natalia became fully awake, taken aback by Kyle. "Excuse me?"

"You heard me bitch. Where the fuck is Mya?" he yelled again.

"First off don't call me a bitch again. Second I don't know. If she is not there, I hope she never comes back to you, you bitch ass nigga."

"You the type of bitch that I would beat just because your fucking mouth is too smart. She ain't have no idea of going anywhere until she started hanging out with your trick ass."

"Wherever she is, I hope it's far away from your insecure, bitch ass. You not a man. You a pussy made bitch."

"Yea, I'll be a pussy that's going to smack the shit out of you, then make you suck my dick."

"Try that woman beating shit over here and that will be the last time your ass ever hit a woman, bitch ass nigga." Natalia said hanging up on him.

Little did Kyle know, Natalia called Taye as soon as she got off the phone with him and told him what he said to her. Taye was livid.

"Nigga, what your chick say to you?" Pete asked Taye as they pulled up to Kyle's house. He saw how upset he was when he got off the phone.

Taye walked right in Kyle's house. Walking up to him while he was sitting on the couch, he stole him right off the back. Not giving him a chance to defend himself, he started punching him in the face, leaving Kyle to wonder what happened.

Slim end up pulling Taye off of Kyle.

"What the fuck Taye?" Pete asked as he pushed Taye back from Kyle. "You lost your mind?"

"What the fuck is your problem nigga?" Kyle said, getting up off the floor. Blood was leaking from his eyebrow and his jaw was starting to swell.

"Don't you ever and I mean ever speak to my woman like that." Taye said moving to beat his ass again.

"You come at me over some fucking bitch? I thought we were better than that."

"Watch your fucking mouth. I sit back and let you treat your woman the way you wanted to but you ain't going to disrespect mines."

Wiping his mouth with the back of his hand, he looked Taye straight in the eye. "Fuck you and that bitch. I know she know where my woman at."

"Keep my woman out your shit. I'm out this bitch. I hope she never come back to you." Taye said with a look of disgust on his face as he walked out the door.

"Fuck him! I don't need him." Kyle said picking up a bottle of vodka and drinking from it.

"Can you let us know why we at your house so fucking early?" Pete asked, still trying to figure out what just took place.

Still drinking from the bottle, he answered, "Somebody kicked my shit in and I can't find Mya ass."

"Damn nigga. We'll get on it and see who knows anything." Slim said.

"Yea do that."

"Shit my ride left me." Pete said.

"Nigga bring your ass." Slim said making his way to the opened door.

As soon as they left, Kyle called a locksmith. He packed some of his shit and left; just in case whoever kicked in his door came back.

Chapter 13

Mya...

It was the day Mya had been waiting for. She was finally being released from the hospital. She took the time and really thought about where she wanted to go with her life. Fully dressed and sitting on the bed, she waited for her friends and family to come and get her. Her hospital room door opened shortly after.

"Good morning baby." Shad said with an Ihop bag in his hand.

Mya smiled at him and said "Good morning Shad."

She and Shad's relationship had gotten stronger since she was in the hospital. After him confessing his love to her, Mya wanted so bad to see where their relationship would lead to, but didn't want to rush into anything just yet. She wanted to give it time.

"I brought you food. I know your ass tired of that diarrhea shit they giving you." Shad said with a chuckle.

Mya rolled her eyes at him. "Shut up. You said you wasn't gonna mention that again."

Moving to her bedside, he leaned down. "My bad baby. I'm sorry. Can I get a kiss?"

"No." Mya said with a pout.

Yesterday after Mya ate her hospital food, they started talking. Out of nowhere, Mya's stomach started to hurt. Jumping up, she made it to the bathroom just in time. She had diarrhea and was beyond embarrassed because Shad was there and could hear everything.

"Don't be like that Mya. I promise I won't mention it again."

"Mention what again?" Scott asked coming in the room with Destiny.

"Nothing." Mya said giving Shad a hard glare.

"Keeping secrets now huh?" Destiny asked.

"Nope of course not." Mya said stuffing her mouth with a pancake. She was in the middle of stuffing her face, when she heard a raised deep voice.

"Really Laurel?" Loyalty said.

"Loyalty I don't have time for your mess right now." Laurel said walking in the room.

Laurel and Loyalty never argued in public, so it was a shock to everyone when they came in the room still arguing.

"Hey sis, how you feeling?" Laurel asked hugging Mya and ignoring Loyalty.

"I'm good. What was that?" Mya whispered for her ears only.

"Nothing you have to worry about." Laurel reassured her.

She was still skeptical, but decided to brush it off. "If you say so."

There was a knock on the door that got everyone's attention.

"Hello Ms. Adams and family." The doctor said walking up to Mya.

"Hey Doc! Please tell me I can leave now." Mya said excitedly.

"Yes Mya you can leave right after you sign your discharge papers." The doctor said with a smile as he handed her the forms.

"My pleasure." Mya said signing the papers quickly.

Once the doctor was out of the room, Laurel cleared her throat. "Did you decide where you want to go?"

Mya looked around the room and smiled. "Yes. I'm going to go to Charlotte with Shad."

Shad smiled bright and winked at her. She didn't want to be in the cold in Boston and she didn't want to intrude on Destiny and Scott. Going with Shad was a good idea because it gave them a chance to get to know each other better too.

"Ok that's settled. Just know Shad, fuck my sister over I'm killing you." Loyalty said with a straight face.

With his hands raised, Shad reassured him, "You have nothing to worry about."

Loyalty and Shad shook hands making sure they had an agreement. Shad and Scott left to go put all of Mya's stuff inside his car.

Loyalty pulled out an envelope full of money and handed it to you Mya.

"What is this for?" Mya asked Loyalty.

"Look, I know Shad is a good nigga, but you my lil sister and you need to have your own. Every month I will send you money. Do what you want with it, but I rather you save it just in case. You won't have to depend on no nigga but family. You feel me." Loyalty said with such sincerity in his voice.

"Yea I feel you. What was that between you and Laurel?" Mya asked worrying about them.

"That nigga Cash keep calling her and it's pissing me off. But it's nothing you have to worry about. We are good."

"Laurel loves you too much to do anything to hurt you."

"I know and I love that woman like crazy, but that nigga just gets under my skin." Loyalty getting angry.

"That's what he wants to do but don't trip. He is a lame."

"That's why you my number one sis." Loyalty said hugging her.

Laurel and Destiny walked back in the room and saw Loyalty hugging Mya. Loyalty had asked them to step out so he could talk to her right quick. Releasing Mya from the hug, he said "Remember I'm your brother. I'm here for you. I want you and your sister happy. I'll do anything for y'all two. Shit, even ma too. She not bad once you get to know her."

"I never thought I would ever hear you say that about my mom." Mya said laughing.

"Shit me either."

"Dang so you don't care about this sister?" Destiny said causing both of them to look at the door.

"Shut up Des. Of course I want you happy, I told that little light skin fucker if he fuck you over I'm cutting his dick off then chop his body up. Who the hell bought you that damn car for graduation?" Loyalty said with a straight face.

"I know. I was fucking with you. You the best big brother everrrrrrr." Destiny said hugging Loyalty.

Loyalty walked over to Laurel. Grabbing the back of her neck and pulling her to him, he kissed her passionately. Before they got carried away, Loyalty pulled back.

"I love you momma." He smiled.

"I love you too papi." Laurel said smiling at him, her cheeks turning pink.

The nurse came in the room with a wheelchair for Mya.

"Oh I can walk." Mya said getting down from the bed.

"It's procedure." The nurse said.

Mya rolled her eyes and got in the chair.

"Can I push her?" Destiny asked, getting excited.

"Sure." The nurse said handing the chair over to her.

Mya looked over her should nervously. "Destiny don't crash me like the last time."

"Girl we were like 10 then." Destiny said. When they were 10 years old, it was an abandoned wheelchair outside their building. They were taking turns pushing each other down the hill and around. Destiny was pushing Mya down a hill and couldn't stop her in time. Mya crashed into a parked car, and had bruised her knees up.

"So, I'm not playing with you." Mya said sternly.

"Hold on." Destiny said taking off running, pushing Mya in the wheelchair.

They were laughing while they ran around the hospital in the wheelchair, going in circles.

"Y'all finished big ass kids?" Scott asked once they made it to the front of the hospital.

"You just mad cause you didn't get a turn." Destiny said sticking her tongue out at him.

"If that's what you want to believe. Save that tongue for later." Scott said winking while pulling Destiny to him.

"So when are y'all heading to Charlotte?" Laurel asked.

Checking his watch, Shad replied, "Now. Well after Mya see Mrs. Adams and I see my mom. I have to get back. I have class tomorrow."

"Get there safely." Loyalty said hugging them both bye.

Laurel and Mya hugged tightly not wanting to let each other go. They both promised to keep in contact and talk at least 3 times a week.

"Shad, take care of my sister." Laurel said as she released Mya.

"I will." Shad said.

After seeing both of their mothers, Shad and Mya got on the high way and headed to Charlotte.

Chapter 14

Mya...

Mya had been in Charlotte with Shad for a little over seven months and she loved it. He treated her like a queen. She met some of his basketball team mates and their girlfriends. He encouraged her to get her GED and apply for college, telling her it's never too late. Since she been there, she got her weight back, and was starting to feel like the old Mya. She was no longer scared for her life, and she talked to her family and friends all the time. Scott and Destiny visited often since they were only about 3 hours away. Just last week when Loyalty called to check on her, he let her know that him, Laurel, her mother and Shad's mother would be down for fourth of July. She talked to her girls too, and they also planned to visit soon. Mya was looking forward to everyone coming down for Fourth of July. She missed everyone terribly.

Mya was sitting in the living room finishing up her online homework assignment when Shad walked in with bags from the grocery store.

"Hey bae, you need help?" Mya asked him.

"Naw I got it. Your man is strong." Shad said carrying the rest of the bags to the kitchen.

Mya got up helped him put the groceries away.

"So what you do today?" Mya asked Shad as they sat on the couch.

"I went and made sure we had all the food for the cookout. Made sure all our folks hotels were booked, because I barely want our mother's staying with us." Shad said.

"Don't do that. You know they miss us." Mya said smacking his arm lightly.

"Bae you know we going to have to give our bed up to them." Shad said. He hated sleeping on the couch. He was too tall for it and his legs always dangled off the end.

"How about we get an air mattress?" Mya suggested.

Smiling at her, he said, "Whatever you want baby."

Even though they hadn't had sex, Shad loved to have Mya sleep under him. He wasn't worried about his mother and Mya's mother staying because he couldn't get any action, he just didn't want to have to sleep separate from Mya.

"Ok, maybe I can convince my mother to stay at the hotel and I'm sure your mom would stay with her." Mya said.

"If you can pull that miracle off, that would be great."

Mya texted Laurel and asked her to call their mother and see if they could stay in a hotel.

"All done." Mya said closing her phone.

"That was fast. What you do?" Shad asked looking at her.

Mya shrugged. "Told Laurel to tell her."

Shad laughed and shook his head. "Took the easy way out huh?"

"Hey my mom can't be mean to the pregnant chick. Who, might I add, will be a lawyer in December" Mya said excitedly.

"Damn I know. Time flies for real. Babe you know how cold it is in Boston. Do we have to go to that graduation?" Shad asked laying his head on Mya's lap while she rubbed his head.

"Yep. Who knows we might need her skills one day." Mya said running her fingers lazily through his hair.

Shad had dosed off shortly after. Easing him up, Mya got up and started to make dinner for them. Shad woke up when it was almost done. Walking into the kitchen, he took in the sight of Mya barefoot and cooking with the skillet. "It smells good in here." he said coming up behind her. Wrapping his arms around her, he leaned down and started kissing her neck.

Mya turned around in his arms and kissed him. They were in a deep passionate kiss, and Mya couldn't help but moan. Just like all the other times when the kiss was getting too good, Shad pulled back. He wanted Mya, but he didn't know if she was ready for the next step yet.

Clearing his throat, Shad stepped away from her. "Let me know when it's ready please." he said, leaving the kitchen.

"Ok." Mya said with disappointment in her voice. Going back to cooking, her phone rang from the counter. Looking at the screen, she smiled when she saw the name flash.

"Hey Des, what's up?"

"Nothing. What you doing?" Destiny asked.

Sighing heavily, she replied, "Cooking."

"What's wrong with you?"

"Shad and I was in another one of those kisses and he pulled away again. Ugh." Mya said frustrated while stirring the cabbage.

"Mya boo. Maybe you need to tell him you want the dick." Destiny said making Mya laugh.

"You are crazy." She laughed.

"No for real Mya. When I was ready to lose my virginity, Scott ass was so clueless until I told him '*aye nigga I'm ready to have sex now.*' Shit we live together." Destiny said.

"I'm not a virgin Destiny. Shit, haven't been since I was 13." Mya said.

"Bitch you a born again. That nigga Kyle do not count. Shit Shad might make you feel like a virgin again." Destiny said laughing.

"I can't take you. But I'll take your advice."

"Yesssssss, call me with details and everything." Destiny said hanging up.

Mya finished dinner and let Shad know. They both were at the table eating when Mya couldn't take it anymore. She had to know.

"Shad, I need to ask you a something?"

He looked up at Mya and gave her his undivided attention.

Looking him straight in the eyes she asked, "Are you attracted to me?"

Shad was caught off guard by her question. He thought she would have seen how attracted he was to her just by the way he stared at her sometimes. "What kind of question is that baby? Yes I'm attracted to you."

"Ok well, why when we kiss, you always pull away from me?" Mya asked. "I mean is it something I'm doing that's wrong?"

It became clear to Shad what the issue was now. "Ohhhh I see." He said, nodding his head. "Baby you are the most gorgeous woman I know. I pull back because I know you went through a lot and I don't want to rush us into a physical relationship. I don't want to seem like I'm forcing you."

"But Shad, I'm ready to be intimate with you. I love you Shad." Mya said, hoping that her eyes told him what she was trying to convey.

Shad stood up from the table and walked over to Mya. Standing in front of her, he caressed her cheek and asked, "You sure you ready?"

"Yes I'm sure." Mya said quickly.

Shad picked Mya up from her chair and wrapped her legs around his waist. Kissing her passionately, he wanted to show her the pleasure he can give her. He sucked on her neck then moved down to her breast, licking and sucking her nipple through her shirt. Placing Mya on the table, he made quick work of her shorts while she took her shirt off. Stepping back, Shad admired her body while she bit down on her lip. Reaching forward, he ripped her underwear from her, leaving her clean-shaven pussy to his view. Cupping her, he gently flicked her clit with his thumb. Mya's back arched up off the table, needing him to keep touching her.

"I've thought about doing this to you for so long." Shad said as he grabbed a chair and sat in front of her opened legs. Pulling her butt to the edge, he hooked her legs over his shoulders and breathed in her scent. Lightly kissing her left inner thigh and moving to her right, he felt her legs starting to tremble. Focusing on his prize, Shad dove straight in and started to suck and swirl his tongue around her clit.

Mya bucked against his mouth and moaned loudly. "Oh my Goooooddnnnessss. Baby what are you doing?" she asked, looking down at his head moving between her legs.

"Finishing up my dinner baby. Relax." Shad said going back to eating Mya out. Sliding a finger inside her, he crooked it over a sensitive spot and felt her tense. Adding a second finger, he rubbed over that spot repeatedly, while still sucking on her clit.

Mya wrapped her legs around his head when the pressure in her lower abdomen became too much. "Ah, fuckkkkkkkk, please Shad. Baby I'm about to…."

Before she could finish her sentence, Shad pinched her clit while still sucking on it, causing Mya to cum back to back. Never had she experienced anything so good in her life. She laid back on the table, exhausted.

"You said you wanted it baby. I'm about to give it to you." Shad said picking her up and carrying her to the bedroom. He placed her on the bed and stepped back to take his clothes off. Mya sat up on her elbows and took him in. She panicked when she got down to his thick dick. He easily had to be 10 inches. Just the thought of him trying to put it inside her made her clam up.

"I'll go slow." Shad said taking in her stuck face. Getting on the bed, he parted her thighs. Touching her pussy, he found that she was still wet. Grabbing the base of his dick, he moved it up and down her slit. Easing inside her slowly, he felt Mya tense up again.

"Relax ma or it's going to hurt." Shad said still pushing in slowly. He closed his eyes against the tightness that he felt when entering her. Mya relaxed and Shad put more in, getting her use to his size. Once she grabbed his biceps, Shad started to stroke faster inside her. Mya gasped, never having felt so full in her life. Getting in a pushup position, he placed her legs over his shoulders before plunging back inside her.

Mya grabbed onto his arms again and moaned out, "Damnnnn baby. Right there. Please don't stop, please."

Shad took his hand and reached in between her legs, finding her clit. Rubbing in fast circles, he felt Mya tense and her legs tremble hard. Squeezing his dick with her muscles, she came on a shout, triggering Shad's climax as he came inside her.

"Damn that was great. I waited years for this." He said as he fell on the bed beside her. Pulling her to him, he kissed her forehead and saw her smiling big.

"I'm so tired and my body hurts." Mya said. She knew she would be walking funny after their session.

"I'll run you a bath." Shad said getting up and walking naked to the adjoining bathroom.

"Thank you baby." She said.

"Thank me for what?" Shad asked looking at her over his shoulder.

"For loving me."

Walking back over to her, he leaned down, "That's a given babe." He said as he kissed her lips.

"Oh and thank you for letting me experience your mouth and making me cum... Hard." Mya said smiling against his lips.

"My pleasure baby. I have a lot to show you then." he said winking at her.

As soon as Shad went to the bathroom and she heard the water running, she wasted no time calling Destiny and giving her the details. "Destiny I have to go girl. I hear him coming back." Mya said hanging up the phone as soon as he walked back into the room. Scooping her up, he took her into the bathroom and gently placed her in the soothing water.

"You not joining me?" Mya asked with a pout when he moved away from the tub.

"I was going to let you relax those muscles." Shad said smiling at her.

"Get in." Mya said moving up so he could get in behind her.

Shad got in and started a whole new session. They had sex all night long all over the apartment. Shad introduced Mya to a whole new level of being pleasure and she loved it. She knew Shad would make her happy.

Chapter 15

Laurel…

"Babe I have to pee and it's hot. Turn the air up." Laurel complained for the 100th time on the ride down to Charlotte. They were just 30 minutes away and she had to pee again.

Loyalty huffed and looked at her, annoyed with her beyond measure. In his truck it was Liz, Shad's mother Rhonda, and Loyalty's mother June who were all sleep.

"Bae, what the fuck you want me turn the air on? Fucking below zero? It's already cold as fuck in here and hold that shit. We almost there." Loyalty said pissed.

"I don't give a fuck what you have to do, I'm fucking hot and I will piss on your fucking seat. Pull the fuck over Loyalty. Dumb ass nigga." Laurel said looking out her window before she was tempted to slam his head against his.

Loyalty kept driving, not paying her any attention. Laurel reached over and punched him in the arm.

"Stop fucking hitting me Laurel." Loyalty said, trying not to swerve.

"Loyalty, pull over and let your woman use the bathroom." June said as she woke up to them fighting.

"Ma we almost there. She can hold it."

"You got her pregnant, and this comes with pregnancy so pull over before I fuck you up son." June said with a smile on her face.

He knew his mom was serious so he took the next exit. Taking a deep breath, he said "I swear these women."

"Oh trust and believe this is your one and only fucking child from me. Bitch ass nigga." Laurel said once Loyalty pulled in the gas station and she got out.

"Get your shit together son. You two laid together and got pregnant, now these are the things y'all go through. If you love her like you say you do, fix it." Loyalty looked at his mother and got out the car and went inside the gas station.

Laurel was feeling much better when she came out of the bathroom. Looking at the Icee machine, she walked right into Loyalty.

"My bad." Laurel said finally looking up and saw Loyalty then rolled her eyes. She tried to go around him but he blocked her path.

"Baby, come here. I'm sorry ma. You know how I get on road trips. I know you pregnant and can't help your bladder. Forgive me." Loyalty said pulling her into him.

"I guess I forgive you." Laurel said not looking his way. Her mind was still on the Icee machine.

"You guess? I can't wait till we get to this hotel. You gonna be screaming you forgive me and how much you love me." Loyalty said smacking her ass and grabbing a handful.

Rolling her eyes, she replied "Whatever. Can you buy me an Icee?"

"Nope." Loyalty said walking away from her.

"I hate you." Laurel said walking to the Icee machine.

"Love you too baby."

Laurel made her drink, got a pickle and hot chips she was craving. The cashier rang everything up, and gave her $15 cash back.

"Excuse me sir, wasn't I suppose to give you money." Laurel said laughing.

"No ma'am. The gentleman that is at pump 2 gave me $20 and said whenever you were done, use that to pay for your things and give you the change." The cashier said smiling at her.

"Thank you." Laurel said taking the change and her things.

When she got in the car, she leaned over and kissed Loyalty.

"You still a jerk." Laurel said as she opened her bag of chips.

"I'm your jerk though." Loyalty said driving off.

__*__*__

Shad...

Shad sat on the couch waiting for Mya to finish getting dressed. They were going to the hotel to see their mother's. They haven't seen them, Laurel and Loyalty since she was released from the hospital.

"Mya, what's taking you so long?" Shad asked walking in the room. She had been getting dressed for over 20 minutes.

"I'm trying to get dressed, but my legs hurt." Mya said lying across the bed.

"Baby really. I told you to chill last night, but naw you want to go all night and morning." Shad said scooping her up into his lap.

"I know, but it was so good." Mya said with her face against his chest.

"Yea I have that effect on women." He joked.

"Don't play with me Shad." Mya said sitting up and glaring at him.

"You know you my one and only. Now come on and get dressed so we can see our mommas." He said, making her stand up.

"Babe can you dress me?" she asked laughing.

Smacking her ass, he looked at her and said, "You know I'm no good with putting clothes on you, just taking them off."

Mya finally got dressed and they headed to the hotel. Shad had the music blasting and was in his zone, nothing could ruin his day. He made love to Mya that morning; he was seeing his mother and all his niggas was coming down to visit.

"Bae, me and the fellas going out to the club tonight. I forgot to let you know last night." Shad said looking over at her briefly.

"Which club y'all going too?" she asked looking at her phone.

"Onyx." He said bopping his head to the music.

Turning in her seat, she asked, "Onyx? The strip club?"

"Yes the strip club ma. You don't want a nigga to go?" Shad asked with a chuckle.

"I really don't but I already know you gonna go anyway." She said with a little attitude.

"What's the attitude for baby?"

Shrugging, she responded, "I don't know."

"Mya look at me." Shad said. When she turned to him, he continued "I am not that nigga. If I go out and chill with my niggas trust and believe I will not do anything to disrespect you. Shit if you want you can go with us. But Micah told me Britt said y'all going out."

"I believe you Shad; it's just going to take time. I ain't know we were going out though."

"Well y'all are. Stop tripping and putting me in that lame ass nigga lane. I love you baby." Shad said reaching for her hand and kissing it.

"I love you too." Mya said smiling at him.

They pulled up to the hotel and Shad helped Mya out the car. As soon as the elevator hit the 4th floor, they both went to their mother's room excitedly.

"Hey ma, I miss you." Shad said as soon as Rhonda opened the door.

"I miss you too son. You look good, all healthy and stuff." Rhonda said pulling him in a hug and looking at him.

"I have a woman that can cook. She makes sure I eat." Shad said smiling.

"Where is my daughter-in-law at anyways?" Rhonda asked.

"She went to see her mother." Shad said sitting on his mother's bed.

"So what you been up to?"

Shad took a deep breath and exhaled loudly. "I just been training and trying to find a job. I feel like less of a man getting my rent paid by my woman's brother. I can provide for both of us."

Shad was living off of work study, scholarships, and refund checks in school to pay his bills. When Mya moved in with Shad, Loyalty told him not to worry about paying for rent and the bills. He was going to take care of everything. Even though Shad didn't like it, he dealt with it because Mya asked him to.

"I understand son, but you need to focus on your basketball career. Loyalty is just trying to help out. Accept the help and when you and Mya are ready to get jobs, then y'all do it together."

"I know ma, but I just feel less of a man. It's just a pride thing."

"Don't feel that way. You are a wonderful man. You are taking care of a woman you loved since I can remember." Rhonda said smiling at him. "On a lighter note, how has it been living with Ms. Mya?"

"It's been great. She cooks, she make sure I'm good, don't complain that much. I don't understand why a lame ass nigga would put their fucking hands on her." Shad said getting upset. He had a relationship with his mom where he could always say how he felt without her judging him.

"That's a weak man. A weak man only does something like that." Rhonda said.

"He messed her up ma. Sometimes I see the insecurity in her. I have to get her to come out the house. But I'm glad I'm the one putting the smile on her face and making her become the woman she wants to be."

"I'm happy for you. What about marriage and grandchildren?" Rhonda asked.

"Dang ma you rushing me." He laughed. "But on the real, I want to marry her in another year. We can worry about kids after we've settled down."

"I'm not rushing you boy. I just want to make sure you make an honest woman out of Mya."

"Come on ma you know me better than that." Shad said giving her a smirk.

__*__*__

Mya...

"I missed you guys' soooooooooo much." Mya said hugging her sister and mother to her.

"I missed you too mami. Look at you looking all good." Liz said happy that her daughter looked healthy and glowing.

"Yea I missed you too lil sis." Laurel said, trying not to cry.

"Have y'all talk to daddy or Mike?" Mya asked.

"I talked to them before we got on the road. They said they are going to call you." Liz said.

"Ok, so how has my nephew been treating you?" she asked, rubbing Laurel's stomach.

"This little boy moves all night and makes me have the worst mood swings ever. Loyalty most likely hates me." Laurel said rubbing her stomach and looking at the floor.

"Girl that man doesn't hate you." She laughed. "You know he worships the ground you walk on."

"So how has it been living with Shad?" Liz asked suddenly.

"It's been great. He is so respectful, caring and I feel so safe with him." She explained as she smiled.

Liz and Laurel looked at her and smiled. They were happy that Mya was finally happy. The Adams women talked and played catch up with each other's lives. A little while later, Shad and Mya got word that all of their friends along with Loyalty and Laurel friends were there. Mya was so excited to see everyone. Leaving everyone, they went back to their place so they could change.

"Shad, did you see my blue wedges?" Mya asked looking in their closet.

"They in the red box on the top of the closet." Shad yelled from the bathroom as he was brushing his wavy hair.

"Baeeeeeeeeee." Mya yelled.

Shad shook his head and walked in the closet shirtless, showing off his nice chest and abs. He walked up on Mya and reached over her head grabbing the shoe box she needed. Mya was staring at his chest so hard, like she was in a trance. She didn't even pay attention when he tried to hand her the box.

"See something you like?" Shad asked, smirking at her.

"Whatever boy. Thank you." Mya said taking the shoe box and waving him off.

Mya looked at her outfit in the mirror and loved what she saw. She wore a tight fitting high waist skirt, crop top and wedges. She straightened her hair which had fallen down her back.

"Come here Mya." Shad said sitting on the edge of the bed. He looked good in his jean shorts, a green polo short-sleeve button down shirt, chucks and a Celtics hat on.

Mya walked to him and stood between his legs. Grabbing her by her hips, he licked his lips as he looked her up and down.

"Baby I want you to have fun. Enjoy your night."

"Ok, you have fun too looking at the strippers." Mya said rolling her eyes.

Shad pulled her in his lap and smiled.

"I promise I won't have fun." He said causing Mya to smile.

"You're beautiful baby and you smell good as shit." Shad said smelling her neck. He let his hands roam up her skirt, while kissing on her neck.

"Ummm." she moaned as she felt Shad getting hard under her.

Just as he was moving her panties to the side, there were loud knocks at the door. Shad sat there with his hand still in the same position and his face buried in Mya's neck.

"Babe they're here." She said, starting to grind in his lap.

"Fuckkkkkk." Shad said getting mad. Now all he wanted to do was throw Mya on the bed and forget about going out.

Laughing at him, Mya got off his lap and went to open up the door. She was greeted by her and Shad's friends. Loyalty and his boys already went to a club and Laurel and her friends stayed in.

"We got the drinks. Let's pregame so we can go out and run this city." Brittany said with a bottle in her hand.

Shad finally came out the room when they were pouring cups. He had a mean mug on his face.

"Fuck your ugly ass looking like that for?" Micah asked.

113

"Fuck you bitch." Shad said mushing his head as he walked past him.

"This nigga must ain't get none." he said, causing everyone to laugh.

"Micah leave Shad alone." Tamara said.

Mya walked up to Shad and kissed his lips. After an hour of doing pregame, everyone was ready to head out.

"Don't be all up on them dusty bitches." Destiny said to Scott.

The girls were going to Bar Charlotte and the guys were heading to Onyx.

"So bitch spill it." Tamara said looking at Mya as she rode in the backseat of the car.

"Spill what?" Mya asked tipsy.

"How was the dick?" she asked, causing an uproar of laughter in the car.

Looking at her with a straight face, she said, "Who said we had sex?"

"Bitch it is all in your walk. Your legs look like parentheses." Brittany laughed.

"Fine! The dick is sooooooo fucking good. I felt like a virgin again and I am hooked already." Mya said blushing.

"Clearly his ass is too." Destiny added as they pulled up to the club.

—*—*—

Shad…

It was packed as the guys walked into Onyx. There were no seats available anywhere.

"Damn man we should have left earlier. Ain't anywhere to sit. I need to get a seat so I can get at least two lap dances." Eric said.

"Nigga shut the fuck up." Scott said then spotted someone he knew. "Yo ain't that Loyalty and them."

"Yep, we are going in their VIP." Micah said getting ready to make his way to the VIP area.

"Naw man. We can't just run up on that nigga shit." Shad said stopping him.

"Really?" Micah said looking at him.

"Look do what y'all want to do, I'm going to the bar."

The rest of the guys walked over to the VIP.

"What up niggas?" Eric said.

Loyalty, Kelly and Moss looked at them and dapped them up, letting them in the VIP.

"Where is my brother in-law at?" Loyalty asked as he looked around.

"That nigga at the bar being a little bitch." Eric said, gesturing over his shoulder to Shad posted at the bar.

Loyalty shook his head as he watched them make it rain on the stripper that was at the table. Getting up he made his way to the bar.

"What's up bro?" He said once he approached Shad.

"Shit just chilling."

"So why you ain't come to the VIP?"

"I'm cool down here."

Loyalty looked at him like "nigga please."

"For real Shad what's the deal?"

"Aight look Loyalty. I appreciate everything you do; paying the bills, making sure my lady good, shit every fucking thing you do. But it is starting to make me feel like I ain't measuring up. My fucking woman will call you if she wants something before asking me." Shad said, ordering another drink for himself and Loyalty.

"Why you ain't say shit nigga. It will be my pleasure to not have another bill on me. But tell me this. You in school, how you gonna take care of school, you and Mya?" He asked with an eye brow raised.

"I'm getting a job."

"Be real Shad. What the fuck a minimum wage job getting you?"

Shad was quiet.

"Right, now I'll make a deal with you." Loyalty said. Shad looked at him and gave him his attention.

"You work for me," Loyalty said, gesturing to himself, "and I'll pay you."

"No disrespect, but you know I'm not no dealer."

"No shit nigga. You studying business, and I need some business property. I need stocks. I need shit to invest my money in because I won't be doing this shit after my son gets here and I get married. So can you be my business manager or do I have to go hire a white motherfucka that I won't trust for real."

Shad looked at him and smiled and said "I got you bro."

"Good, so after this weekend start working on different proposals and shit. I want something solid real soon." He said giving him firm handshake.

"Aight, bet. I'll get right on that then."

"Now let's go get drunk and get some lap dances." Loyalty said steering him to the VIP table.

"Naw I'll watch. Mya ass will not kill me if I smell like any of them hoes."

Loyalty laughed at Shad and added "Oh believe me I know, her sister the same damn way."

Chapter 16

"I'm hungry as fuck." Destiny said as they walked out the club drunk.

"Yo, it's a waffle house by where we staying at." Mya said excitedly.

"Let's go." Brittany said walking to the car. The girls were more than hype to be getting some food. As they pulled up at the waffle house they saw Laurel, Melanie and Tiara at a table. Walking inside the restaurant, Tamara made her way over to their table.

"What the hell y'all doing in here at 3am?" Tamara asked hugging them and taking a table behind them.

"Pregnant ass right here wanted Waffle house." Melanie said pointing at Laurel who was digging into her food.

Everyone started to order when then they heard loud voices coming through the front door. Some of the girls recognized the men off back, since they were their boyfriends.

"Hey baby." Moss said to Tiara, clearly drunk.

She frowned her face up and said "You drunk as hell ain't you?"

"Nope I am not drunk." Moss said laughing then added "I'm fucked up baby."

Pushing him from out her face, she said, "You irritating. Go sit over there somewhere."

"What's up ma?" Loyalty said kissing Laurel softly on the lips.

"Nothing. How was the strip club?"

"The same. Give me a bite." Loyalty said eating a piece of her pecan waffle from her fork.

Shad picked Mya up and sat her on his lap, eating off her plate.

"I was going to eat that Shad." She whined.

"Sharing is caring baby." He said eating her last piece of bacon.

Watching him drink all her juice, she got mad. "Really Shad?"

"What? You want me to buy you some more?" he asked while licking his lips.

Rolling her eyes at him, she folded her arms and huffed. "No I'm ready to go home."

"Let's go. You gonna let me hit tonight?"

"Nope and how are we getting home? You didn't drive."

"I went and got my car. And why I can't get any?" he asked, squeezing her thigh.

"You ate all my food." Mya pouted

"I'll reorder your food." Shad said calling the waitress over.

"Naw let's pay and leave."

Shad picked up Mya's ticket and passed it to Loyalty.

"Here bitch." Shad joked.

"Naw nigga. Didn't you just complain about not paying her bills and shit? You got it BITCH."

Shad starting laughing. "I'll start after this weekend but you got this one. We out." Taking Mya out on his arm, they walked to his car and drove home. Mya kicked her shoes off by the doo when they made it home and went straight to the bathroom. On the other hand, Shad had passed out on the couch; his liquor finally catching up to him.

"Baby." Mya said walking in the living room and seeing him half on the couch. Grabbing her phone, she took some pics of him then helped him undress and make it to their bedroom.

As soon as Mya closed her eyes, she heard "Mya baby."

"Yes Shad." She asked with her eyes closed still.

"Ride me ma."

"Babe you are drunk and half sleep." She said. She wanted to have sex, but she figured he was out of it.

"Man, come here." Shad said grabbing her around the waist and pulling her on top of him. Since Shad was already naked and Mya didn't have any underwear on, it made for easy access.

She wasted no time straddling him, grabbing his dick and lowering herself onto him. She rode him in slow motion then sped it up when Shad grabbed her waist. She rotated her hips and rocked back and forth. Shad had a nice grip on her and was enjoying watching her. He sat up fully, causing her to lie on her back. Grabbing her legs, he placed them on his shoulders and went to work on her pussy. Mya screamed his name when he kept hitting her spot. Not wanting her to cum yet, he turned her over and made her get on her hands and knees. He watched Mya rotate her hips as he grabbed his dick and rubbed the head against her lips. Calming her, he pushed his dick into her in one single thrust, making her gasp. Stroking her deep, he showed her pussy no mercy. Every time she tried to move away from him, he would pull her back by her hips. Pushing her into the mattress, he swiveled his hips, feeling Mya tense up. He knew she was about to cum when she started throwing it back on him. Feeling her wetness on his thighs, Shad came inside her. Collapsing to the side, he grabbed her and pulled her against his chest. They both fell asleep wrapped up in each other.

Mya woke up to the ringing of Shad's phone. With her eyes still closed she grabbed it.

"Hello."

"I know y'all asses are not still sleep." Rhonda, Shad's mother said.

"No ma'am we up." Mya said pushing Shad.

"Shit Mya, stop pushing me. I'm trynna sleep." he said turning over.

"Mya come open up this damn door." Rhonda said.

Her eyes got big as she took in what his mom just said. "Y'all at our door?"

"Yes. We have been knocking for a while. Come open the door. These bags are heavy."

"Ok, I'm coming." Mya looked down and realized that she and Shad were still naked.

"Shad get your ass up. Our mothers are at the door." Mya said popping him on the ass.

"What?" Shad said looking at her with blood shot red eyes.

"Put some clothes on. Our mothers are at the door and got bags." Mya said finally dressed in shorts and a shirt.

Shad jumped up and grabbed a pair of basketball shorts. Looking at the clock, he realized it was 9am. Smacking his teeth, he went to open the door.

"Bout time boy." Rhonda said giving him a glare.

Shad took the bags from them without saying good morning and placed them in the kitchen. He hated to be woken up out his sleep and he was still tipsy.

"Hold the hell up." Rhonda said. Everyone stopped and looked at her. "I know I raised you better than that Shad Miles Jackson. Don't get jacked up in front of your girlfriend."

Shad looked at his mother, rolled his eyes and said "Good morning ma, good morning momma Liz, good morning momma June." Giving them all hugs.

Rhonda hit him in the stomach hard and said in his ear once he bent over holding his stomach "Don't play with me again son. I love you."

Mya finally came out the room and spoke to everyone and gave them hugs and kisses. She looked at Shad and noticed he was holding his stomach.

"What's wrong baby?" Mya asked walking up to him. She hoped he wasn't about to throw up on the carpet.

"Ma punched me in my stomach. That shit hurts." he said with his face screwed up. He stood up quickly and ran to the bathroom, throwing up all the liquor from last night.

"Go take care of that drunken fool Mya. We got this in here." Rhonda said gently pushing her in Shad's direction.

"Ok." Mya went to their bathroom to make sure he was good while their mothers prepped the food for the cookout.

"You okay baby?" Mya asked as she sat on the side of the tub.

"No." Shad said laying his head on her lap. She stroked his head, until she felt him drifting off.

"Shad lets go get in the bed." he got up off the floor and walked to the bed. They both got in the bed and went back to sleep until 1pm. After waking up, they got dressed for the Fourth of July cookout. Walking to the pool area, the grill was full with food, the pool was packed, the drinks were being poured, you can hear the laughter, and everyone was having a good time.

"So how is my nephew?" Mya asked Laurel as she sat next to her on the pool side as they got a tan.

"He is active. Moving like crazy." Laurel stated, enjoying the sun kissing her skin.

Before Mya could say anything else, she looked at who was coming through the doors of the pool area.

"Oh my goodness." Mya said running to them hugging them so tight.

"Hey sis! You look so good." Natalia said.

"Hey sis." Taye said hugging Mya.

"I didn't know y'all were coming down." She yelled, almost crying.

"We wanted to surprise you." Natalia stated.

"This is great." Mya said as Shad walked over.

"Glad y'all made it. What happened to being here last night?" Shad asked them.

"Mr. busy man right here had some shit to do."

"Always about the paper." Shad said laughing.

"Hey, what can I say? My new bosses all about the money."

Taye and Kyle hadn't spoken since he fought him for disrespecting Natalia. He started working for Loyalty, Kelly and Moss and was making triple the money he had been when he was with Kyle.

Everyone was so relaxed and having a great time. All Mya could do was thank God for bringing her closer to her family and friends again. As the fireworks went off, she hugged Shad's waist when he leaned down and kissed her forehead. "I love you so much."

He kissed her lips and said "I love you more."

Chapter 17

2 years later

It's been two years since Mya and Shad have been together and they couldn't have been happier. They moved from their apartment and were living in a 4 bedroom house. Shad graduated from college and was now in grad school getting his Master's in business. He was working for Loyalty and getting paid good money. So far he got some restaurants, clubs, bars and stock in Loyalty, Moss and Kelly's name. Mya was taking online classes for fashion design. She always wanted to create her own style and she was doing great at it.

Loyalty and Laurel had their son: Trust Major Wills. He was the most adorable baby ever. He was a mixture of Loyalty and Laurel. Even though he still hustled, he slowed it down a lot. A year after Trust was born, they got married. She was escorted down the aisle by her father and brother on a private island. Once Laurel graduated from law school, she went to work on getting her father and brother out of jail and she did. Now she and Loyalty were working on opening up her own firm. Big Mike made a promise to all his kids and wife that he would never disrespect their mother again. He had been sticking to that promise ever since. Lil Mike was on another mission: to find his Ex Amber and fuck her life up.

"Mya wake that ass up." Shad said smacking her on her ass. When he came out the bathroom, all he had was a towel on.

"I'm up." Mya said sitting up stretching, making her shirt rise over her growing belly. She was now 7 months pregnant, but looked like she was due any day. She and Shad were expecting a baby girl in August. They were getting ready to head to DC to celebrate her father's 50th birthday celebration. Neither Shad nor Mya haven't been back to DC since she was release from the hospital, so everyone was shocked when she said they were coming to the party.

"Good morning my beautiful ladies." Shad said kissing Mya then kissing her stomach. He was so excited when he found out she was pregnant. He wanted to marry her right then and there, but she told him to wait until they were done with school.

"Babe I don't think I want to go to DC anymore." Mya said looking down.

"Ain't nothing going to happen to you. Don't I always protect you?" Shad asked.

"Yes."

"Well nothing is going to change now." He said smacking her on her ass then grabbing it pulling her close to him.

Mya undid his towel and kissed his lips passionately as his hands roamed her body. Before she knew it, she was naked as well. Shad sat down on the bed and let Mya climb on top of him. Seating herself fully on his dick, she began to slide up and down.

"Baby, my legs are getting tired." Mya whined, feeling her legs start to shake.

"It's ok baby. I got you." Shad said as he grabbed the back of her thighs, helping her bounce up and down. As he started to get more into it, he picked up his pace and starting stroking upwards, hitting Mya's spot repeatedly.

"Fuck, I'm about to cum bae. You are so fucking tight." He said, trying to hold off until she came.

"I'm cumming bae. Shit, I love you." She yelled as she reached her peak.

"I'm right behind you baby. Wait for me… You feel so good." he moaned.

"Aww daddy" Mya said repeatedly.

"Baby I'm cumming," Shad responded as he released inside her, feeling her climax around him. Picking her up and laying her on her side, Shad cuddled up behind her while placing a hand over her stomach. They both fell asleep shortly after.

__*__*__

Mya was excited to see her family and friends, but was praying she didn't run into Kyle. She knew if she saw him it wasn't going to be pretty. After riding for six hours, they pulled up in front of Loyalty and Laurel's new house.

"This is nice." Mya said seeing her sister house for the first time in person.

"Yea it's fly ma. Let's go in. It's hot out here." Shad said wrapping his arm around her as they walked up the front porch.

Knocking on the door they heard a little voice asking "Who is it?"

"It's your aunty Mya." As soon as Mya said that, Trust opened up the door and jumped in her arms.

Trust loved him some Mya. He would get on his mother's phone and Skye her and when they visited Mya, he followed her everywhere.

Trust hugged her tightly. Leaning back in her arms, he looked her in the eyes and said, "Aunty you here. I miss you."

"I missed you too my handsome nephew."

"Wanna see my room? You can shleep with me. I got a big boy bed now." Trust said excitedly.

"Dang little man. You don't see your uncle standing here." Shad said giving him a fake glare.

Trust looked at him and smiled. Reaching over to him he said, "Hey Unc Shad."

"Nope I don't want your hugs man. Get off me." Shad said pushing him back into Mya's arms and going in the house. Scrambling to get out of Mya's arms, Trust started to run behind him. Hearing his little feet behind him, Shad took off running through the house.

"Aye aye aye. Trust why you running through the house?" Laurel asked, coming out the kitchen with Loyalty behind her.

"That's because my big kid is running from him." Mya said shocking them both when they saw her.

"Myaaaaaaa! When you get here? Give me a hug." Laurel said running over to hug her sister.

"Nigga you can't just be walking in people house like that." Loyalty said giving her a hug.

"My nephew opened the door because his freaky parents were having sex in the kitchen." She said with a hand on her hip as she pointed to them.

"It's my damn house and my wife." Loyalty said going to sit on the couch. Mya followed him and plopped down, holding a hand to her bulging stomach.

"Here sis, smell my finger." Loyalty said to Mya, putting his finger under her nose.

"Stop Loyalty! That is so fucking nasty." Mya said pushing his hand away from her face.

"Fine then." Loyalty said putting his finger in his mouth and sucking it, while winking over to his wife.

"You are really nasty." Mya said with a screwed up face.

Before he could respond Shad and Trust made their presence known.

"What's up nigga?" Shad said about to give Loyalty some dap but Mya stopped him.

"No baby don't touch his hands." She said causing Shad to look at Loyalty's outstretched hand.

"What's on your hand bruh?"

"Just some left over juice." Loyalty said shrugging like it wasn't a big deal.

"Bruh, that's nasty as fuck." Shad said laughing.

Smacking her teeth Laurel said "He was actually squeezing the lemon for the butter sauce. He has lemon juice on his hand. We can't do anything with this hyper ass boy running around."

Mya punched Loyalty in his chest, ready to smack him upside the head next.

"What you do that for? I told you to smell my hand. You would have known what it was then."

"You play too much. I was about to say we staying with mommy."

Laurel laughed at her sister. "Whatever. You know you wouldn't stay with mommy if we paid you to."

"You damn right."

"Naw babe we getting a hotel. We don't want to invade anyone privacy." Shad said.

"Nigga shut the fuck up. Y'all are staying in the guest house. No questions." Loyalty said.

"Whatever nigga. Let's eat cause a nigga hungry."

That night they had crabs, shrimp, mussels, baked potatoes, corn on the cob, and salad.

"I'm so stuffed." Mya said as her and Shad lay in bed. The guest house looked like an actual house, with two bedrooms, a full bath and kitchen.

Shad pulled Mya's hand to him, "Come here." He said, as he rubbed her stomach.

"So what's the plan tomorrow?" she asked.

"I have to go see my family. What about you?"

"Tomorrow can be family day. Oh babe you have to meet my dad." Shad and Big Mike never met but talked on the phone quite a bit.

"Sure." Shad said kissing her lips. After they prepared for bed, they fell asleep, with Mya wrapped securely in Shad's arms.

_____ * _____ * _____

"Aunty, Unc wake up. Wake up! Wake up shleepy heads." Trust said standing on the side of the bed.

Mya moved her wild hair out her face and looked at her handsome nephew. "Good Morning."

"Good morning aunty. Did you sleep good?"

"Yes baby. How did you get in here?" she asked, squinting against the morning sun.

"I opened the back door and walked in here." Mya shook her head and chuckled. Now she saw why Laurel always had high locks on the door. That boy could get in and out of everything.

"Let's go see your mommy. She might be looking for you." Mya climbed out of bed and got some shoes to put on. Fixing her hair in a messy bun and brushing her teeth, she followed Trust out the guest house.

"Mommy looks who I got." Trust said when they got in the kitchen.

"Trust how many times do I have to tell you do not leave out this house without me knowing." Laurel said, slightly raising her voice to him.

"I just went to get aunty." He said looking down at the ground, about to cry.

"Come here. I'm not mad. I just don't want anything to happen to you." Laurel said squatting down and hugging him.

Laurel and Mya made breakfast and talked. Mya missed this time with her sister and nephew so much. By time everyone ate and got dressed, it was the afternoon. The ladies and Trust were going to Liz house, Shad was going to his mother's house and Loyalty was going to work. Riding with Laurel, she noticed how much DC had changed and loved it. Pulling up at their parent's new house, Mya was surprised that they had actually moved to Maryland.

"How did y'all convince ma to move out here?" Mya asked.

"Well dad actually did that. It just so happened that dad had some money stashed up and that's how they got this house." Laurel stated pointing to the large American Craftsman style house.

"Dad is so low down. He didn't know ma struggled, leaving you to get a job and Mikey to hustle."

"I don't know what that nigga was thinking. Let's go in and see them." Laurel said, getting out the car and getting Trust.

Mya was more than excited to see her parents and brother after being away from them.

Chapter 18

"What do you want Destiny?" Mya asked once she answered her phone. She was lounging on the couch watching TV. Her father's party was tomorrow and today all she wanted to do was relax. She had been visiting people all day.

"Don't be answering the damn phone like that. Any who, what your pregnant ass doing?"

"I am currently laying on the couch watching TV waiting for my man to come on so we can go to the mall."

"Which mall? Me and Scott will meet y'all because this nigga owe me some shoes."

"I don't owe you shit." Scott yelled in the background.

"We just going to Pentagon City. I want to go to their Forever 21, even though I can't fit shit right now."

"Girl you 7 months. You better buy shit that you would look good in after you have that baby, because I know that body gonna be snatched."

"I swear something is wrong with you." She laughed. When she looked up, Shad came into the room looking edible. "Here comes baby daddy now. We about to leave out."

"I'll meet you at Macy's." Destiny said hanging up.

"Babe you better stop staring at me like that." Shad said smirking.

Walking up to him, she kissed him on the lips. "You know you fine right?"

"Thank you. Glad you think I'm fine. You ready to go baby momma."

"Yep. Let's go baby daddy. Scott and Destiny meeting us there."

"Cool."

When they made it to the mall and met up with Destiny and Scott, they went to almost every store. They were buying clothes for the baby, clothes for themselves and stuff for Trust. After taking a trip to the car to drop off their stuff, Mya's stomach rumbled.

"I'm hungry. Let's go to the food court." Mya said.

"What you want to eat baby, so I can get it?" Shad asked with an arm around her waist.

"Oh my! I want everything. I want 6 chicken tacos from taco bell, a large fry and 10 piece chicken nuggets from McDonalds. Oh and a slushy from Auntie Anne's." Mya said naming everything she wanted.

"What the fuck?" Scott asked. He was trying to figure out how she was storing all this.

"Don't come for me Scott. I'm eating for two." She said, holding up 2 fingers laughing.

"That's your excuse for making my brother stand in fifteen lines?"

"Yep."

"Leave my sister alone and go stand in line with him cause I want some tacos and an almond pretzel." Destiny said pushing him in the same direction.

Scott rolled his eyes and went with Shad to get their food.

"So how does it feel to finally visit home after two years?" Destiny asked as they sat down at a table.

"It's not bad. I saw my parents and Mikey. I've missed them so much."

"How my boo doing? I can't wait to see him tomorrow at the party."

"You such a creep." Before Destiny could respond a little girl around the age of 3 accidently bumped against them.

"I'm sorry." She said looking up from her toy on the ground.

Mya and Destiny smiled at her. Mya looked at her closely and thought she looked so familiar.

"It's ok sweetie." She said.

"Kyla, why are you bothering these ladies?" Mya and Destiny looked at the woman with sunglasses on and knew exactly who she was. It was Ashley and the little girl was Kyle's daughter Kyla.

"I was just saying sorry mommy."

Ashley finally looked up at the women and mugged them. "Mya."

"Hello Ashley. Long time no see." She said with a smile on her face.

"I know you." Kyla said to Mya.

Mya smiled down at her and said "I know you too."

"Daddy has a picture of you. He said you is his wife." Kyla said innocently.

The mention of Kyle put a bad taste in her mouth.

"That's nice of your dad but I am not his wife."

It happened so fast and Mya's breathing grew once she heard the voice that used to give her nightmares.

"Ashley you over here talking and shit, didn't I tell your ass to sit at that table over there." Kyle said walking up to Ashley. He still stood 6'4, with a full thick beard. He gained a lot more muscle and was still good looking.

"I know but your daughter bumped into them and I was coming to get her." Ashley said pushing her sunglasses up on her face. Mya knew he was beating her ass now.

Kyle looked at Destiny and Mya. He did a double take when he saw Mya and smiled hard. "Mya... baby where you been at? I been losing it for two years that you was gone. I looked everywhere for you." Kyle said happy to see her but Mya was scared as shit. She wanted Shad to hurry back. Now she was regretting wanting all of that food.

"Baby talk to me. You look good." He said, taking a step towards her.

"She don't have shit to say to you, and she ain't your fucking baby." Destiny said stepping in.

"Same ole Destiny. I hoped my brother dropped your ass." Kyle said mugging the shit out of her.

"Your brother knows a good woman when he sees one, unlike an insecure, lame ass nigga like you."

"Don't no one want to hear your ass." Kyle said, then turned his attention back to Mya "I miss you baby. Come back to me. We can work everything out."

As Kyle begged Mya to come back to him, Ashley stood there with her heart breaking. Even after being away for years, Kyle was still desperate for her.

Shad and Scott were walking back over with their food, when Mya saw them. She exhaled a sigh of relief. Shad put the food down quickly and looked at Kyle who was trying to get in Mya's space. He looked Kyle up and down. Mya stood up and hugged Shad so tight, almost on the verge of tears.

"You ok baby?" Shad asked, kissing her forehead and hugging her.

"Yes, I'm fine. I'm glad you're here."

Kyle noticed her stomach at that moment and he was getting angry at the sight in front of him. He looked over to his brother who looked like he wanted to spit in his face.

"What's up little brother?"

"Kyle." Scott said in a monotone voice.

"Damn bro, it's like that. We brothers, we blood." Kyle said with his arms outstretched.

"Take it how you want man. We been stopped being brothers."

Kyle laughed then looked at Shad, "So you think you won?"

"Nigga it's not a competition." He said, looking at him like he was dumb.

"We will see who she ends up with." Kyle said with confidence.

"I'm not about to entertain you man. Keep it moving." Shad said not in the mood for Kyle's childish act.

Kyle smiled at him and looked at Mya. "I love you ma. I'll see you soon." Kyle said walking off, leaving Ashley standing there with their daughter.

Mya was scared shitless but had to warn Ashley. "Ashley." She called over to her, getting her attention.

 "Leave him now. The longer you stay, the worse it gets. Take Kyla and leave him. He will destroy you. He almost killed me but I had people to help me. I'm trying to help you."

Ashley fixed her sunglasses and said, "Thank you but I'm fine. Unlike you, I know how to handle him."

Feeling like she would have to realize it on her own, Mya said, "Ok."

Before Ashley walked off, Scott said "Ashley you going to introduce me to my niece?"

She rolled her eyes and said "Kyla go speak to your uncle Scott. That's your father's brother."

Kyla smiled at Scott. Leaning down, she gave him a hug as he wrapped her arms fully around her.

"I saw your picture at grandma's house." Kyla said looking at him.

"I saw yours too. Here is my number, you call me whenever you want to talk, and it don't matter where I am at I will come and get you." Scott said handing her a card with his information on it.

"Ok Uncle Scott. I love you."

"I love you too." Scott said as he watched Ashley grab her hand and walk off to catch up with Kyle.

"Sis you good?" Scott asked Mya when he turned around to her.

"I'm fine." Mya said picking at her food. She was no longer hungry.

"He real lucky his daughter was right here. I swear I want to beat the fuck out that nigga. No disrespect to you fam." Shad said to Scott.

"None taken at all."

"How about we leave? That nigga just ruined my shopping fun." Destiny said.

They all agreed. As Mya and Shad walked to the car, Mya held onto him extra tight. Shad took notice of it and didn't like it. He wanted to kill Kyle for scaring Mya. He made sure she was in the car then got in.

"Babe you ok?" he asked after riding in silence for 5 minutes.

Mya just nodded her head. Shad couldn't take the silence, so he pulled over on the high way.

"Mya look at me." Mya looked over to Shad with unshed tears in her eyes. He could tell that she was truly shaken up. "Don't let that nigga fuck up your happiness. When you sad and hurt, I'm sad and hurt. I'm hurting right now baby because I don't see your smile. Fuck that nigga. He don't have shit to do with our lives. We have a baby girl on the way and we about to get married. Don't let him steal our happiness."

Mya smiled at Shad and said "How am I so lucky to have a man like you?"

"Shit, I'm the lucky one. I love you Mya Adams."

"I love you Shad Jackson."

"When we get back to the house, you can show me how much you love Me." he said leaning over and kissing her softly on the lips.

She pulled on his bottom lip with her teeth and replied, "Oh I will daddy."

Pulling up, they noticed no one was home and went straight to the guest house. Mya pushed him on the couch as soon as they walked to the living room. Getting on her knees, she pulled his shorts and boxers down in one move, letting his dick spring free. Without waiting, she took him into her mouth and started to suck hard, hollowing her cheeks to take more in.

"Shit Mya." Shad loved the way Mya was working her mouth. She had a firm grip on the base, while she stroked and sucked on the tip of his dick. She was doing things with her tongue that was driving him crazy. "Fuck, Mya baby get up before I cum." he said, trying to pull Mya up but she kept going. "Shittttttttttt." Shad yelled as he let his load off in her mouth.

Mya got off the floor while wiping her mouth. She stripped out of her sun dress and underwear, standing in front of him naked. Shad got himself together and couldn't take his eyes off of her body. Pregnant and all she was still fine as hell. His dick got hard and he was ready to put a hurting on her pussy.

"Come here mommy." Shad said pulling her towards him. He laid her on the couch and spread her legs wide, burying his face between her. He ate her out so good. Mya gripped his head and pulled him deeper. The way his tongue was moving was driving her crazy. Shad moved his tongue lower and started eating her ass, while flicking his fingers over her clit. Mya came suddenly. No matter how much she tried to get away, he wouldn't let her go. She came again, and it was so much that her body felt drained.

"I don't think I can move baby." she said, trying to catch her breath.

"Get some energy because I'm ready to fuck now ma." Shad said stroking his hard dick and taking in her glistening skin.

Mya looked at his long, thick dick and licked her lips. She was tired but got her second wind when she saw him grasping his dick.

"I'm ready papi." That's all Shad needed to hear. Getting between her still spread legs, he went deep inside of Mya. He took his time, making sure to give it to her long and deep. Each stroke told her how much he loved her.

"Te quiero tanto, amor. Fuerte!." (I love you so much, baby. Harder!) Mya rarely spoke Spanish even though her mother made sure all her kids knew it. She had the urge to speak it to Shad and he loved it, even though he didn't know what she said.

"Shit ma you trying to make a nigga bust speaking like that. Turn over." Placing a pillow under her stomach, Shad turned her over and was hitting it harder like she wanted from the back. He pulled her hair, making her lean back into him. He kissed her passionately, not missing a stroke. All you could hear were moans and skin clapping together.

"Fuckkkkkkkk Shad baby don't stoppppp."

"Throw it back ma." Shad said moaning, feeling his balls tighten up.

Right when they both were about to cum, the front door opened. "Mya let's go around the … Oh my goodness." Laurel said finally looking up and seeing Shad and Mya having sex.

"Get the fuck out Laurel." Mya said to her sister who was just standing there.

"Shit my bad." she said, slamming the front door as she ran out.

Shad never stopped fucking her during the interruption, which she was grateful for. They were both nearing their climax.

"You want me to pull out baby?" Shad asked sensing her mood change.

"No, I want you to finish." She moaned loudly.

Shad continued but sped it up, making both of them cum. Out of breath, they went to shower and got dressed, heading to the main house.

"You enjoyed the show sis?" Mya asked coming in the kitchen finding her sister on the phone.

"Girl I'll call you back. Your nasty ass cousin and my sister just walked in." Laurel said to Melanie hanging up the phone.

Mya rolled her eyes while Shad looked through the refrigerator and got them a water.

"Yo, where is Trust and Loyalty?" Shad asked Laurel.

"They out with Mason, Kelly and Moss. I came to see if Mya wanted to go around the way."

"Oh cool. Well I'm about to go hang with my niggas."

"Wait, you leaving me?" Mya asked, turning to look at Shad.

"Babe you gonna be with your sister. I'll see you later. Have fun with your girls." he said pulling her into him and kissing her, while grabbing her ass.

"Y'all mad nasty." Laurel said.

"Whatever. I know you and Loyalty do worse." she said pulling away from Shad.

"Love y'all and be safe. I'm out." Shad said leaving out the house.

Laurel and Mya got in her car and headed to their neighborhood. Pulling up, they saw that everyone was outside; all Mya friends, Laurel friends, Cash and his crew, Mikey, and Lord. Mya was so excited to see Lord. She missed him.

"Damn what's up Mya? Hey baby." Cash said, speaking to Laurel.

"Fuck off Cash." Laurel said.

"Hey Cash." Mya said.

"Damn baby it's like that? I still love you."

"Yo, didn't I tell you to stop talking to my sister. You gonna make me fuck you up out here." Mike said getting mad.

"Chill man, I was just fucking with Laurel." Cash said not trying to get into it with him. Everyone knew that nigga got crazier since he got out.

Mya and Laurel walked off to their friends.

"Lorrrrrddddddddd." Mya yelled hugging him tight.

"Hey lil sis. Look at your ass, all pregnant and shit." Lord said looking at her and her round stomach.

"I know. How come I ain't hear from you in a minute?"

"Man, shit overseas is crazy, and Keya ass always working like crazy. So I been mad busy." Lord explained. After graduating from college, instead of going pro in the states, he got picked to play in Spain. Keya got a chance to study abroad over there for med school. They only came home once in a while.

"Did you and Keya elope yet?"

"Nigga shut the hell up. Ain't no one eloping. Did you and Shad elope?" he asked, switching it back to her.

"Maybe we did, maybe we didn't." Mya said causing him to laugh. She missed this. It felt like old times.

Chapter 19

Kyle...

"Yo, shut the fuck up." Kyle said to Ashley. Ever since they left the mall, she had been talking about how he was acting when he saw Mya.

"Who you talking to Kyle? I'm not that bitch Mya. You know I fight back."

Kyle punched her so hard in her mouth, causing it to bleed. Not giving her a chance to retaliate, he punched her again and again. "Don't call her a bitch again. She more of a woman than you would ever be." Kyle said punching her again.

He was about to give her another blow when he heard his daughter. "Daddy, my movie gone off." Kyla said looking at her father stand over her mother while she held her face.

"Ok princess. Let me finish talking to mommy and I will put another movie on."

"Ok." Kyla said looking at them again, then walking back in her room.

Kyle looked at Ashley and said "You listen to me bitch. Don't you ever and I mean ever disrespect Mya. You would never be her. You know she is the only woman that I love and have my heart. If I ever hear you say something disrespectful about her again, I'll make sure I knock some of your teeth out."

Ashley just looked at him. She knew how Kyle felt about Mya, but that never stopped her from being jealous that she couldn't have his heart. She gave him a child and stood by his side through it all, for her to only get nothing in return.

"I'm out bitch. Clean yourself up." Kyle said heading to his daughter's room and turning on another movie. Leaving out the house, he got in his car and drove off to the trap house where he met Pete and Slim. Over the last two years, things changed and Kyle was a boss now. He had people running for him and didn't have to get his hands dirty like he use to when he was a corner boy.

"What up niggas?" Kyle said stepping in the house.

"What up fool? I ran into your punk ass brother and his friends today." Slim said.

"Fuck that nigga. Where you see him at?"

"He was around the way." He replied.

"Nigga I thought you missed your brother." Pete said rolling up his blunt.

"Shut the fuck up." Kyle said taking the blunt out his hand. He finished rolling and lit it. After taking the first hit, he had an idea. "Let's do a ride out."

"Who we blasting on?" Pete said always ready to fire his guns.

"Hmmmmmm… that lame ass nigga Shad." Kyle said thinking about how he wanted to put a bullet inside of Shad for taking Mya from him.

"Hold up. You want to shoot up your own hood?" Slim asked laughing.

"Yea, I have a target."

"Bruh you straight tripping. I'm not firing on my own block nigga." Slim said leaning back on the couch.

"Fuck you then nigga. Let's ride Pete."

Pete and Kyle got in their unmarked car they used for drive-bys.

"Tell me the real reason why you trying to fire on that weak ass nigga?" Pete asked.

"I saw Mya today."

"Wait. Where you see Mya at? Her ass just up and disappeared last I thought."

"Nigga don't I know. I looked for her ass for two years. But I saw her at Pentagon. Man she look good as fuck. Only fucked up thing is her ass pregnant by that nigga Shad."

"You lying. Mya loved your ass too much to get pregnant by his wack ass."

"Who you telling? She was acting scared to talk to me and shit. I ain't like that shit. I'm going to see her again and we going to be back to normal. She gonna have to get rid of that fucking baby though. I'm not raising another nigga kid." Kyle said, already picturing them back together.

"Where she staying at?"

"No clue, but word around town her pops big Mike is having this big party. Imma show up and get my woman back."

"That's what's up man. You and Mya are meant to be together." Pete said slowing down as they pulled up on their block, ready to fire it up.

Kyle looked out the window until he saw who he was looking for. Climbing in the back seat, he rolled the window down and hung out of it. He cocked his gun, tapped on the hood signaling for Pete to push it. Kyle let rounds off looking at everyone run. He was aiming to kill Shad.

Pete rounded the corner and Kyle got back in the car.

"I got that nigga." Kyle said unloading his gun.

"Good." Pete said heading back to the trap.

—*—*—

Shad ...

"Who the fuck was that?" Shad asked after the shooting stopped.

"Man, I don't know. Everyone good?" Scott asked his boys.

"Yo, Shad you bleeding son." Eric said looking at the red stain on his shirt.

"What? No I'm not." Shad said looking down and noticed blood on his shoulder. Touching it, he knew that he had only been grazed by a bullet.

"Where is Micah?" Scott asked.

Eric looked on the side of the building and saw Micah laying there holding his stomach. They all ran to him. Taking his arms from around his stomach, they saw the bullet hole and the blood seeping out. Everyone quickly moved into action.

"Micah don't die. Man don't die." Eric said while Scott called the paramedics.

Micah was breathing but he was going in and out, slowly losing consciousness.

"Call Tamara. She gonna be worried if I don't come home." Micah said weakly.

Eric pulled his phone out and dialed Tamara's number.

"No Eric, Micah cannot stay out all night." Tamara said in the phone laughing when she answered.

Before Eric could respond, the paramedics were pulling up.

"Yo, over here hurry up. He is losing a lot of blood." Scott yelled in the background.

"Eric, who is losing a lot of blood?" Tamara yelled in the phone.

Eric hung up the phone so he could make sure the paramedics were handling the situation.

While Scott, Eric and Shad were making sure they were taking care of Micah. Tamara was having a panic attack.

"What is wrong with you?" Tiara asked her sister.

"Eric just called me. I thought he was asking if Micah can go somewhere. Then I hear the paramedics and Scott saying he losing a lot of blood. I don't know who he was talking about."

"Oh my God." Mya said, picking up her phone to call Shad. She didn't get an answer so she tried again.

Scott sent Destiny a text saying they were heading to Howard University hospital.

Eric and Scott made sure that Micah was good then got in car and followed the ambulance.

"Shad why you ain't ride with them? Your ass bleeding all over my seats." Scott complained.

"Nigga it was an in and out I'm fine. All I need is stitches."

"You are still bleeding on my shit though."

They all got out the car and sat in the waiting area. Shad checked himself in as well to get stitches for his graze.

"Did you call Micah mother?"

"Yea, I did." Scott said, and then his phone rang. Seeing it was Destiny, he answered immediately. "Yeah babe."

"Where are y'all?"

"We in the emergency area."

"Ok."

Destiny, Tamara, Brittany and Mya came.

Mya looked around and saw that Shad wasn't sitting there.

"Where is he?" Mya said about to cry.

"Calm down Mya. Look Shad was shot, but the bullet grazed him. He went back to get stitches. Micah was shot as well and he lost a lot of blood. We don't know what's going to happen." Scott explained.

Tamara started to scream. Eric held her while she cried on his shoulder.

After sitting there for an hour, Shad came out. Since his wound was minor, he was released right then and there. They still had to wait for Micah to get out of surgery.

"You scared me." Mya said hugging Shad.

"I'm sorry. They just came out of nowhere shooting."

"Did you see him, Shad?" Tamara asked.

"They doing surgery sis. Just pray."

They all— including Micah's mother— stayed at the hospital until 3am. Loyalty came and checked on them, made sure everyone was fine, and brought their cars to them with the help of his boys.

"Brown family." The doctor said as he walked into the waiting area.

Everyone stood up and waited.

"Micah is stable. The bullet entered his upper abdomen and grazed his left lung. We were able to get the bullet out but the next 48 hours are the most critical. He is now in a room resting."

"May we see him?" Tamara asked anxiously.

"Only two people." Tamara and his mother went.

Shad drove back to Laurel and Loyalty's house with an aching shoulder and a lot on his mind. He was wondering who would open fire on the block. Shad looked over at Mya and saw a worried looked on her face.

"Mya what's wrong?"

She just broke down crying. He pulled into the drive-way and parked the car. Pulling her into his lap, he wiped her face. "Talk to me Mya."

"I thought I lost you. I was scared to death when you weren't sitting there with Scott and Eric."

"Stop crying. I told you I would never leave you. I'm right here."

"I have a bad feeling that something bad is going to happen baby. I think we should leave."

"Your pops party is tomorrow. We can leave after that."

"You promise?"

"I promise."

Even though his shoulder was hurting, he picked her up and carried her into the guest house and held her all night.

"Shad, I love you. Please don't leave me."

"I love you too Mya. I'm not going anywhere." he said kissing her forehead.

Mya drifted off to sleep.

Chapter 20

Mya ...

Mya woke up in Shad's arms and easily got out the bed to release her bladder. She walked out the bathroom and looked at the patch that was on his shoulder. She said a quick prayer. For some reason she couldn't shake the feeling that something bad was going to happen. Picking up her phone, she checked on Tamara who said that she was good and Micah was doing better. Mya made her and Shad breakfast before going to talk to her sister and Loyalty to let them know they were leaving after their father's party.

"Where you been at?" Shad asked as he came out the bathroom, seeing Mya sitting on the bed with their plates.

"I went to the house to tell Loyalty and Laurel that we are leaving after the party. How is your shoulder?"

"It's ok. Just a little sore. Nothing too painful." Shad said sitting on the bed digging into his food.

"I talked to Tamara. She said Micah is up and he is ok."

"Thank God. He had me scared."

"Who shot at y'all?"

"To be honest baby I have no idea. Shoot all of us hardly be home so I don't know."

"Do you think it was Kyle?"

Shad laughed and said "I had my thoughts it was him but then he wouldn't be dumb enough to shoot up his own block and with Scott out there."

She nodded, "Yea he wouldn't try and harm Scott."

Shad went back to eating and noticed the worried look on her face again.

"Babe stop worrying, we good. Give me a kiss."

Even in her worried state, Shad always knew how to make her smile. She leaned over and kissed his lips.

"What time we have to head to the party?"

"Well I have to go help set up, so I have to head out at 3 but you don't have to be there until 7, unless you want to help set up." Mya said smiling at him.

"Nope. I'll go visit Micah and then make my way there."

Sticking her tongue out at him, she said, "You suck."

"Don't be mad because you have to set up. Your ass better take a nap. You know how you are."

"I know but I'm not tired." She said, eyeing him.

"Is that your way of hinting you want some dick baby?" Shad asked with a smirk.

"You so nasty."

"And you already know this. Do you want to be put to sleep or nah?"

"Come on Daddy." Mya said smiling at him.

Shad wasted no time pulling her shorts and underwear off and pulling her shirt over her head. He spread her legs and licked his lips, ready to feast on her. He took his time as he ate Mya out. He wanted to make sure that she came at least three times before he took his shorts off. Easing inside of her wet pussy, he moved slow, sped up, slowed down again then sped up. It was driving Mya crazy. He was rotating his hips as he went deeper inside her. He pulled out all the way, leaving only his tip in. Mya was losing control and was soaking his dick from the way he was fucking her. He placed her on all fours with a pillow under her stomach and he went in on her pussy. She tried to move away from him when the pleasure got too much. Grabbing her hips, he pulled her back to him while rotating his hips on a deep thrust.

"Where you going baby?"

"Fuckkkk Shad. Slow down baby."

Shad went slower, watching her ass jiggle as he slow stroked her. His stroking caused her to curse him in Spanish. Mya started to throw it back on Shad. They were moving in sync, when they both came long and hard together.

Shad pulled out and Mya lay on her side, out of breath and yawned.

"You sleepy now?"

"Shut up." She said drifting off to sleep.

When she woke up, it was 1:30. She dragged herself out the bed and looked at Shad who was knocked out. She went and got in the shower letting the hot water relax her body. When she got out the shower, Shad was still asleep. Shaking her head, she began to get dressed. She made sure to put her and his party outfit to the side. After getting dressed, she packed their bags so they can head back to Charlotte.

Mya's phone rang. Picking it up, she saw that it was her sister.

"I'm dressed Laurel. I'm coming."

"Ok I'll be in the car." Laurel said hanging up.

Mya tapped Shad but he didn't wake up. She knew he was a hard sleeper.

"Baby get up." Mya said pushing him harder.

"I'm up. What's up?" Shad said looking at her with one eye opened.

"I'm about to leave. I packed our bags already, and don't forget to bring my outfit."

"Ok, I'll see you in a little." Shad said turning over going back to sleep.

"Really Shad?"

"What now?"

"Nevermind." Mya said getting off the bed.

"I'm playing baby. I love you." He said, pulling her back to him and kissing her fully on the lips.

"You play too much. I love you too."

__*__*__

Mya and Laurel pulled up at the venue where the party would be held and was met by their mother, aunts and Destiny.

"Can y'all explain to me why I'm here helping set up?" Destiny asked.

"Because you are the best honorary sister, and plus your best friend will not be much help." Laurel said with a pout.

"Take my title back." Destiny said causing Laurel and Mya to laugh.

"No can do boo." Mya said putting her arm around Destiny's shoulder as they walked around the venue.

By 5PM, they were almost finished with everything. The decorations were almost done, the food was nice and hot, and the DJ was there to set up.

"Stop eating all the food." Liz said to Mya.

"But ma, we hungry." She whined while pointing to her stomach.

"Mya that is your third plate. Go over there and help them." Liz said pushing her out the kitchen.

Mya walked over to Destiny and Laurel.

"Do y'all need help?"

"Nope, plus your ass can't get up here. Shad will kill us."

Liz came from the kitchen and said "One of you need to go to the store and get some bags of ice."

"I'll go since you won't let me eat and I can't help with the decorations." Mya said rolling her eyes.

"Ok. Don't take long." Liz said.

"I won't. Laurel let me see your keys."

Laurel reached in her pocket and handed her keys over. As soon as Mya adjusted the seat in Laurel's car, she pulled out her phone. Seeing she had a missed call from Shad, she dialed his number.

"What's up baby-momma?"

"Ugh don't call me that. What do you want boyfriend?"

"Ugh don't call me that." Shad said mocking her.

"You so silly."

"I know, but I'm leaving the hospital about to head to the party. Shit I forgot your outfit."

"What? How you forget my outfit Shad." Mya yelled.

Shad started laughing. "I'm fucking with you baby. What you doing?"

"I'm heading to the store to get the ice."

"Want me to meet you at whatever store you going too?"

"Nope." She said, popping the P. "Just be there when I get back so I can change."

"Yes ma'am."

"Ok, let me get off this phone. Love you"

"Love you too." Shad said hanging up.

Mya had to go to three different stores because the other stores were sold out. Standing in line at the 4th store, she was praying they hurried up. She was hot and ready to get back to the party. Suddenly she was having a bad feeling in her stomach.

"How you doing today? Would this be it?" the cashier said ringing up her bags of ice.

"I'm fine, thank you. Yes this would be it."

"Your total is $17.38."

Mya was looking in her purse for her money when she heard "I got it."

She looked to her left and there stood Kyle.

"Here you go sir. Have a great day ma'am." The cashier said brightly as she handed him the change back.

Without saying anything, Mya took her cart and walked quickly out the store. Kyle ran and caught up to her.

"Damn baby why you treating a nigga like that." he said grabbing her arm.

Pulling her arm from his grasp, she yelled, "Get the fuck off of me Kyle."

"What's up with you?"

"I just want to leave."

"Well before you leave tell me this. Why did you leave me?"

Mya looked at him like he was stupid. "You should know why I left you."

"I apologize for hitting you." He said with sincerity in his voice.

"Kyle, New Year's Eve, I tried to commit suicide, but I was unsuccessful as you can see. Thank God it was unsuccessful because every day I wake up and I am happy. I am finally happy and I have a real man to thank for that. Now I really would appreciate it if you left me alone." Mya said walking away towards the car.

"So you trynna say I wasn't a real man?" Kyle asked, getting angry following her.

"No you weren't. You were an abuser, weak, insecure, and a coward." She answered, getting closer to the car.

Mya didn't even make it three feet away from Kyle before her vision went dark.

__*__*__

Shad...

"What store did y'all send Mya too?" Shad asked Destiny while he held her dress.

"She just supposed to be going to get ice. She should have been back soon."

20 more minutes went pass with no answer to her phone. He started to get nervous and was in deep thought when he heard his name.

"Where is your fiancé? The party about to start and she still not back with the ice?" Liz asked, taking in the stress lines on his face.

"I'm going to call her again ma." He called her phone again and still didn't get an answer.

"Loyalty." Shad called out.

"What up nigga?"

"Do umm, Laurel have onstar or something in her car?" Shad asked rubbing the back of his neck, showing how stressed out he was.

"Yea why?" He asked wondering what go Shad uneasy.

"Mya ain't answering and I have a bad feeling. I need to find my woman."

"Let's go." Loyalty said heading to his car.

Before they could head out the door, Laurel stopped them.

"Where are you two going? The party is about to start."

Loyalty didn't want to spook his wife so he said "We just running to the store. We'll be right back."

"Ok, don't be too long."

"We won't baby." Loyalty said kissing her.

As soon as they got in his car, he did the tracker to find Laurel's car. The tracker led them to the grocery store that was a few streets over. They pulled up beside the truck and exited the car. Next to it were melted ice bags, which put them on high alert. Shad walked around the car and noticed her purse was under it.

"What the fuck? Where the fuck is my wife?" Shad yelled.

"Shit. It has to be cameras or something." Loyalty said looking around the parking lot.

They ran in the store and ask for the manger.

"How may I help you gentlemen?" The manager asked as he came to the front.

"Look, I need to look at your cameras that are pointing to that parking lot." Loyalty said pointing to the space behind him.

"If you two are not cops, I can't do that."

"Look I'm trying to be calm and nice. But I ain't no fucking cop, my fucking wife is missing, and her truck is there along with her purse and the ice she was buying." Shad said stepping up to the manager.

"You still need to be a cop." He said, taking a step back.

Loyalty pulled his gun out and grabbed the man by his collar. "Look man, we really trying to be nice. All I need is to see the security cameras so I can know who the fuck took my little sister." Loyalty said then looked at his name tag that read Greg. "Greg, if I don't find my sister, I will literally kill your whole family. Now I can blast your head right here in front of everyone, see the cameras for myself, then go murder your family or you can be a Good Samaritan and let us see the cameras."

Greg was nervous and by the look of Loyalty and Shad he didn't want to test them, so he took them to where the cameras were. They watched the tape from two hours ago. They saw Mya pick the ice up and get in line. They saw a male figure approach her and pay for her stuff. Shad zoomed in on the man but he kept his face down like he knew the camera was on him. They watched Mya walk out the store and the guy grab her. Shad and Loyalty were getting pissed. They watched as words were exchanged, and then they saw her walking off and the guy hitting her in the back of her head with a gun. As she dropped the guy scooped her up and finally looked up. Shad saw red as the man's face became clear: Kyle.

"I'm going to kill that nigga." Shad said beyond angry.

Loyalty watched and noticed he parked next to Mya which meant he was following her.

"He was following her." Loyalty said taking a deep breath and running his hand over his face.

Shad was pacing back and forth with a look that would kill.

"Thank you Greg." Loyalty said as he got the license plate number.

"Should I call the police?" Greg asked.

"No we are going to take justice into our own hands." Loyalty said then looked at a fuming Shad. "Let's go bro. We have to go hunting."

Shad just looked at him and walked to the truck. They drove both cars back to the party. Even though they didn't want to worry them, they had to let the family know that Mya was kidnapped. Walking back into the party, Laurel took one look at Shad and knew something was wrong.

"What's going on?" She asked when they stopped in front of her.

"That nigga Kyle took Mya. Baby I have to go." Loyalty said.

Before she could say anything Mikey, Moss and Kelly came over noticing the tension on Loyalty's face.

"I'm going with you. He took my fucking sister." Laurel cried.

"What the fuck is going on?" Mikey said as he and the guys caught the end of what Loyalty said.

Loyalty explained to them what happened. About Kyle stalking her, following her in the parking lot, knocking her over the head and then taking her. Before he could even finish, Mikey went into beast mode.

"Look we wasting fucking time. I have to find my fucking wife." Shad said, heading to the exit.

No one else said anything. They all went to Loyalty and Laurel's house and strapped up. Hitting the streets, they knew that once they found Kyle, it was over for him.

Chapter 21

Mya...

Mya woke up to her head throbbing. She looked around and realized she was in a room, but unaware where. She was trying to remember the last thing that happened before she blacked out. Kyle popped in her head immediately. Even though her head was hurting, she refused to die without trying to save her and her baby.

"Help... Help... HELPPPPPPPP!" Mya yelled.

Kyle opened the door and looked at her. "Baby calm down. I didn't mean to hit you that hard. I was just trying to make you calm down so we could come home."

"This is not my home Kyle and stop calling me baby." she said giving him a look of disgust.

Tilting his head, he looked at her and said, "I'm going to take it that it was the hit to the head that got you talking crazy to me."

"Please just let me go." She pleaded.

"You don't get it do you? You belong to me Mya. The only way you will be able to leave is in a body bag."

"This is kidnap! Why are you keeping me here against my will?"

"No!" He yelled. "It's bringing my woman back home, not kidnapping and don't say that shit again. Now get some rest because tomorrow we going to find a way to get rid of that nigga seed you carrying." He said, closing the door.

Mya started to cry. Rubbing her stomach in a soothing manner, she spoke to her daughter growing inside of her "Don't you worry about nothing

. Mommy is not going to let anything happen to you. I will kill him before I let any harm come to you. We are going to get away from him. I promise you baby girl"

Kyle failed to realize that Mya wasn't the same weak, young girl. Now she was a strong woman and willing to fight for her life. It wasn't just about saving her life. She had to save the life still growing inside her. She looked around the room for anything that would help her. She found a rusty nail and was ready for anything he was going to bring her way. She didn't sleep all night because she didn't know when he was going to come for her. She didn't want to be taken by surprise. She had something in store for him this time around.

—*—*—

Shad...

Shad was riding around looking for anyone that knew Kyle. He was getting frustrated until he saw Pete. He pulled his car in front of Pete and jumped out.

"Nigga what's your problem?" Pete yelled.

"Where your boy at?"

Pete laughed and said "Come on lil Shad. You not about that life, just get back in your car and leave."

Shad felt like he was disrespecting him. His anger had reached its peak. Punching Pete in the nose, he followed up with a punch to his stomach and a left hook to his jaw.

"Where is he?" Shad asked still beating his ass.

"I don't know man. I haven't seen him since yesterday." Pete said trying to protect himself.

"Yesterday did y'all shot at us?" Shad asked stealing him again. He knew that they had to be behind the shooting.

"That was his idea."

"You almost killed my friend." Shad said pulling his gun out and aimed it at his head. He looked around the dark streets and it was clear. He shot Pete in the head at close range. Blood went everywhere. He got up and went back to his car and drove off. Only thing on his mind was getting Mya back. He would take out anyone that came in his way of that. His phone rang bringing him out his zone. "Yea."

"Where you at bro?" Scott asked.

"I'm on the hunt."

"Let Loyalty and them handle this. This ain't you man."

"I gotta go." Shad said hanging up.

His phone rang again. Getting impatient, he answered quickly. "What?"

"Where you at?" Loyalty asked.

"I'm leaving 23rd place. I caught that nigga Pete. He's gone."

"Location so I can have someone to clean it up."

Shad told him where Pete's body was and told him he about to pull up at his house.

Loyalty came outside and saw all the blood on Shad.

"Yo, I think you should just chill and let us handle this." He said, taking in the look on his face.

"Naw, I'm going to murk that nigga. You don't understand. If anything happens to her, I will lose it. She is my everything. I swear to God if something happens to her, I'm killing anybody he loves." Shad said. Tears of anger were streaming down his cheeks. He made a promise that he would find Mya, no matter what it took.

Loyalty knew his brother was hurting and understood where he was coming from. Not caring about the blood, he pulled him in a hug, reassuring him that Kyle's time had ran out.

Chapter 22

Mya…

She didn't know what time it was when she heard the bedroom door opened, but she knew it was dark outside from the tiny window that shield close. She was nervous but she wasn't going to show it. Kyle came in and sat on the bed, rubbing up her leg. "Get your hands off of me."

"Or what?" he said. Before she knew it, Kyle reared back and punched her in the jaw, causing her to drop the nail in her hand. "I swear you love disobeying me. So are you going to let me get some or am I gonna have to take it."

Mya didn't say anything as she tasted her own blood, but that didn't stop her from trying to get out his grip. After struggling with trying to get her sweat pants down, he resulted to beating her. Mya was making sure to fight back and cover her stomach. He was raining blows on her when she saw an opening and kicked him in his nuts. Kyle grabbed his balls giving her enough time to grab the nail. Not waiting a second more, she stabbed him in the eye, causing him to scream out and reach for the nail.

"Agggrrhhhhh you bitch." Kyle screamed

Mya struggled to get up from the bed but she managed. In so much pain, she ran to the door. Throwing it opened, she took in her surroundings and saw what looked like the front door ahead of her. Opening it, she ran outside. She didn't know where she was but she could hear cars through the darkness. She ran for her life, as she heard Kyle still screaming behind her.

"I'm going to kill you, you bitch."

"Myaaaaaaaaa, I'm going to fucking kill you."

"Baby come back, I didn't mean it, I won't hurt you."

She saw a gas station across a highway. She looked back and heard Kyle's voice yelling for her. Taking off running across the highway, she prayed she would make it. Holding her stomach with both hands, she dodged cars that were honking and swerving to avoid her. Once she made it to the gas station, she saw that there were a lot of cars at the pumps. Pain crippled her body but she yelled out "Help" before she collapsed to the ground.

A car full of girls saw her collapse. Taking in her form, they knew she needed help and ran to her.

"Oh my God it's Mya." Keya said getting closer and realizing who it was. Without a second thought she took her head into her lap.

"What is she doing out here?" Lord's cousin Heaven asked.

Keya looked her over and noticed blood on her face and some swelling. Looking lower, she saw that blood was seeping through her pants. "I don't know but we need to get her to the hospital. Call Lord now."

They all got her in the car and drove to Ft. Washington hospital. Heaven was in the front on the phone when Lord picked up. She handed it over to Keya. "Hello. You done partying already?" Lord said once he answered.

"Bae, call Shad. We found Mya at the gas station." She said frantically.

"What you mean?" Lord said.

"She was beaten badly. We are taking her to Ft. Washington hospital.

"Ok." He answered, already getting in his car and dialing Shad's number.

—*—*—

Shad...

Still in bloody clothes, Shad was sitting in the guest house on the couch. His phone rang and he just picked it up.

"Yea." He answered, sounding exhausted.

"I don't know what the fuck is going on but my girl said she found Mya at a gas station beaten." Lord said.

Shad immediately stood up and ran out the guest house. "Where she at now?"

"They are taking her to Ft. Washington hospital."

"Ok." Shad said hanging up as he ran in the main house.

"We got to go!" He yelled when he opened the door. "Keya found Mya. They are taking her to hospital." Shad said already making his way to the front door.

"Shad! Go shower and change. You can't go to the hospital like that." Loyalty said. He knew that police would be all over him.

"I don't have fucking time." Shad said impatiently.

"You will go to jail with blood on you. Go fucking shower." Loyalty said stern.

Shad thought about it and it made sense. He showered fast and changed into some shorts and a black V neck. The three of them headed to the hospital, where they met everyone else.

"This shit is history repeating itself." Shad said.

"Just pray." His mother Rhonda said.

"Fuck praying ma, I swear to God if something happens to her." Shad said pounding his fist on the empty chair next to him, causing it to echo loudly.

"Look, I know you upset but you need to calm down."

Before Shad could say anything else the doctor appeared.

The doctor came out and said "Adams family."

They all stood up and the doctor was shocked to see so many people.

"How is my wife?" Shad asked walking up to the doctor.

"She was beaten pretty badly; there are a couple of fractured ribs." Before the doctor could finish Shad interrupted him.

"How is our baby?"

"She is fine. She came out healthy after having an emergency C-section. We're going to keep her for a little while to monitor her since she is premature."

Shad broke down crying. Wiping his face, he asked, "May I see them both?"

"You can only see them for a few. Ms. Adams is heavily medicated and the baby is getting some test ran on her."

"Ok." Shad said following the doctor.

They went to Mya's room first and Shad couldn't help but be thankful that she was alive. He kissed her on the lips and told her he loved her. The doctor took him to where the babies were. Without the doctor pointing the baby out, he knew which was his daughter, she had a head full of black hair and was the perfect mixture of him and Mya.

Walking back to the waiting area, he smiled with tears in his eyes. "They both are fine."

Everyone was so excited. What was on Shad's mind now was making Kyle pay.

Chapter 23

Mya...

Mya opened up her eyes and wondered where she was. She looked left and right and nothing looked familiar. She looked at her arm and noticed an IV.

"Where am I?" She thought to herself.

Mya started to panic and as soon as she was about to attempt to get out of the bed, a nurse walked in.

"Ms. Adams, I see you are awake." The nurse said walking over to her.

"Where am I?" she asked still confused and with her vision a little cloudy.

"You are at Ft. Washington Hospital."

"What am I doing at the hospital?" she asked.

"You were brought here after your friends found you passed out. You were pretty beaten up." The nurse said keeping it real.

Mya laid her head back on the pillows, lost in her own thoughts, and then she touched her stomach. Looking down, she became alarmed when she didn't feel her baby kicking or moving.

The nurse read her mind and said "You delivered your baby girl."

"Is she ok?" Mya asked starting to cry.

"She is doing fine." The nurse assured her.

"Can I see her?"

"How about I bring her to you after you talk to the doctor?" The nurse said.

"Ok, thank you." Mya said relaxing in the bed reflecting on what happened to her yesterday. As soon as she closed her eyes, the doctor came in and asked her some routine questions. He told her that she had an emergency C-section and that she had some fractured ribs. The baby was healthy weighing 6 lbs 8 ounces and was 16 inches.

Mya and the doctor looked at the door when they heard it opening, revealing Shad. He smiled weakly at Mya, while she gave him a big smile.

Going to her bedside, he hugged her and kissed her forehead repeatedly. "I'm so sorry baby. I'm supposed to protect you and I failed."

"It's not your fault Shad. I love you. You didn't fail me, because of you I was able to get away. I fought back. I thought of you, but more importantly, I thought of our baby girl." Mya said crying.

"I love you so fucking much Mya." He said, embracing her and breathing in her scent. They were wrapped up in each other when the nurse wheeled their daughter in. She didn't want to interrupt their moment but she knew they would want to see their baby.

"Excuse me." They both looked up and smiled when they saw the basket.

The nurse walked over and gave the baby to Mya. She counted her fingers and toes, kissing her cheeks gently. The baby opened her eyes and Mya was head over hills.

"She has your eyes baby." She cooed.

Shad looked at their daughter and fell in love all over again.

"Do you guys know what you want to name her?" the nurse asked, smiling at the family.

"Miracle Summer Jackson. What you think Shad?" Mya asked looking up at him.

"I love you it. This really was a summer of miracles." Shad said kissing Mya and Miracle.

Chapter 24

A week later

Mya and Shad didn't go back to Charlotte yet. They were waiting for Mya's week follow up appointment. Since Miracle was here, they threw a baby shower once she was release from the hospital. Shad was happy since he already had the baby's room together in Charlotte.

"Come on little momma go to sleep for daddy." He said, while rocking Miracle gently.

"You want me to get her?" Mya asked raising her head from the pillow.

"I got her baby, get some rest. You have a doctor's appointment tomorrow."

Mya didn't argue with him. She turned over and fell back asleep. Shad finally got Miracle to go to bed and was able to get in the bed himself.

Shad closed his eyes but was awaken a short time later by a text from Mikey telling him to come outside. He knew that meant they found Kyle. He eased out the bed got dressed and met them in the car.

"You ready?" Kelly asked.

"Yep."

They rode to the stash house Kyle was staying at. Picking the lock, they eased inside and split up to find him. Mikey found him in the bed with some chick, sleeping like they had no worries in the world.

"I got him." Mikey said causing him and the girl to jump up.

The girl looked at Mikey and he smiled when he realized who it was: Amber.

"Damn. A nigga really is sleeping good after he tried to kill my little sister." Mikey said laughing.

"What you talking about?" Kyle asked trying to play dumb.

"Look I'm going to handle her," he said pointing to Amber. "I have been looking for you for a minute now baby, you one hard hoe to track down. Y'all make sure y'all beat the shit out of him, matter of fact." Mikey said punching the shit out of Kyle causing his lip to bleed.

"Now y'all can beat his ass." Mikey stated then grabbing Amber by her hair and dragging her out the bed.

Shad passed his gun to Loyalty and said "Come on, I been waiting to beat your ass."

"Lil Shad, you not serious. Get real nigga." Kyle said, getting out the bed, after shaking off Mikey punch. Before he even took 2 steps, Shad was all over him. He hit him so hard you could hear the breaking of his nose and ribs. That caused Kyle to scream out in pain. He stomped him out when he fell to the ground and didn't stop his assault until Kyle was bloody and hardly recognizable.

"Give me the gun." Shad said.

Loyalty passed him the gun and stepped back.

"Bye bitch." Shad said emptying the gun on him, making sure he wasn't breathing anymore.

They walked downstairs to see Amber slumped over the couch and Mike counting money.

"Nigga really?" Loyalty said with a straight face.

"What? This is the money she stole from me." Mike said shrugging.

"Y'all wild. Give me the guns." Moss said so he could make them disappear.

"Shit this was fun." Kelly said putting gas around the house so he could set it on fire.

"Just get me back home before my woman wake up." Shad said, already missing Mya. He was finally able to close a chapter in his life.

Kelly lit the house on fire and said "Nigga we all need to be home."

As they watched the house catch fire, they walked to the car and pulled off. When they dropped Shad off, he went inside the guest house and showered quickly. Getting back in bed, he pulled Mya to his chest and placed an arm around her waist.

"Is he gone?" Mya asked sleepily.

Shad smirked and said "I can't get anything pass you huh?"

"Nope."

"Yes he's gone baby. Now let's get some rest. I love you Mya Jackson." He said kissing her neck.

"I love you too Shad Jackson."

Epilogue

Unknown...

I laid back on this hard ass fucking mattress, thinking and counting down my last two years until I'll be a free man again. Eight years down and two more to fucking go.

"Inmate you have a visitor." The guard yelled.

Shit, I haven't had a visitor since I came in this bitch. I wonder who the fuck this could be.

"Inmate I don't have all fucking day."

I looked this fat motherfucker up and down and still took my time. Shit I don't have shit but time so I don't mind wasting his. Ignoring all the niggas that was saying what's up and shit, I was trying to figure out who the fuck was here to see a nigga after eight years. Walking to the visitor room, I looked around and my eyes landed on my mother. As soon as I saw her, I knew she was bringing me bad news. Shit when a nigga got knocked she told me, "I ain't raise no animals", and she won't be visiting me like I'm a fucking animal either. Her ass meant that shit too.

I gave her a big hug nonetheless. I missed my dukes.

"Hey ma, I miss you." I told her as we sat down at the table.

"I miss you too son, but you know I hate to see you like this. Locked up with all these... people" she said shuddering.

"I respect it ma."

"How are they treating you in here?" she asked. Her eyes were weary for some reason. I could tell my mother was holding something in and it was weighting heavy on her.

"Ma, stop stalling. Tell me what's up?"

Exhaling softly, she looked me right in the eye and said, "Your little brother was murdered."

"Say what ma?" I asked feeling like I heard her wrong.

"He is gone baby." My mom told me with tears running down her face.

I tried to calm my anger but that shit wasn't working. The more I inhaled and exhaled the angrier I got. I hit the table so hard it caused the whole visitor's room to get quiet and look at me.

"Inmate one more time and you in the hole."

"Who did it?"

"We don't know baby. We are leaving it to the cops to solve. No one has any leads."

"The cops? The fucking cops? Ma they ain't gonna do shit." I said, raising my voice to her.

"We have to have faith baby." My mother tried to grab my hand.

"Faith? Fuck faith ma. I'll be out in two years. That's all that matter. I'll handle it myself."

"Don't talk like that baby."

I pulled my hand from hers and said "I love you ma but I gotta go."

"Don't have a revenge mentality son." She said, tears swimming in her eyes. I just looked at her and walked away. I was too angry to think about anything but revenge for who killed my little brother. All I know is when I touch down after my release;

I'm going to get this revenge for my brother. Whoever did it better pray the police get them before me because I'm coming for their whole family.

The End....

TRUE GLORY PUBLICATIONS

IF YOU WOULD LIKE TO BE A PART OF OUR TEAM, PLEASE SEND YOUR SUBMISSIONS BY EMAIL TO TRUEGLORYPUBLICATIONS@GMAIL.COM. PLEASE INCLUDE A BRIEF BIO, A SYNOPSIS OF THE BOOK, AND THE FIRST THREE CHAPTERS. SUBMIT USING MICROSOFT WORD WITH FONT IN 11 TIMES NEW ROMAN.

www.ingramcontent.com/pod-product-compliance
Lightning Source LLC
Chambersburg PA
CBHW070704280626
47159CB00022B/1975